MW00478824

SINGE

www.chellebliss.com
CHELLE BLISS
USA TODAY BESTSELLING AUTHOR

Publisher © Bliss Ink August 3rd 2021
Edited by Lisa A. Hollett
Proofread by Read By Rose & Julie Deaton
Cover Design © Chelle Bliss
Cover Photo © James Critchley

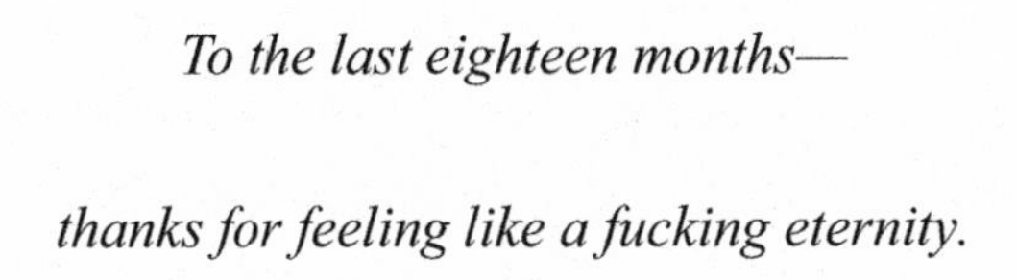

To the last eighteen months—

thanks for feeling like a fucking eternity.

PROLOGUE

CARMELLO

I CRAVED FORGIVENESS. NEEDED IT MORE THAN THE AIR I breathed.

Spent eleven years trying to find it, too.

First, I did good deeds for anyone I could, but after a short amount of time, the small measure of happiness they provided me wore off.

Next, I tried a relationship, thinking settling down with someone would fill the darkness caused by my actions. But that didn't work. I got hooked to a crazy-ass bitch who tattooed my name on her body after forty-eight hours, and any thoughts of future relationships fizzled.

Awkward doesn't even begin to describe the entire breakup with that chick.

After that, I gave up on anything long-term, deciding to find forgiveness somewhere inside me by the simple act of enjoying life—coupled with therapy, of course.

I was smart enough to recognize I needed help.

My therapist was male so there'd be no chance I'd have her body bent over her desk, seeking more than advice. I went to his office once a week for six months, paying thousands of dollars to him, and I still felt the same each time I walked out the door.

Empty.

I knew I didn't cause my former girlfriend's death. It was ruled an accident because no one can control Mother Nature, especially not a group of asshole deer bolting into the middle of the road.

But deep in my mind, back in the darkest recesses, I still blamed myself for not swerving the opposite direction and not forcing her to put on her seat belt.

We were young and dumb. Death felt like something that couldn't touch us…until it did.

Some people deal with their guilt and grief by getting lost at the bottom of a bottle of booze or pills. I'd never been one to dull the pain without there being some pleasure in it too. There was no pleasure in waking up with a hangover or fiending for another fix.

I tried to find my redemption another way.

One full of satisfaction instead of numbness.

Women.

But a man cannot find salvation buried deep in pussy.

I tried. Lord knows I tried.

All types of pussy, too.

Tight pussy.

Loose pussy.

Easy pussy.

Hard-to-get pussy.

Nameless pussy.

Faceless pussy.

Pussy in every position.

None of it mattered.

They were all the same.

Each encounter ended with emptiness.

I couldn't go on this way.

Each year ticks by, no better or worse than the one before.

I am wasting my life.

It may have been one hell of a ride, but it is still completely unfulfilling.

Most of my cousins have moved forward, even my twin brother, while I am stuck somewhere in the past, floating through each day without an anchor.

My life needs to change, or else I'll end up alone, watching those around me revel in their happiness.

1

I TAKE A LONG SIP AS THE CLOCK STRIKES MIDNIGHT. The crowd cheers when the confetti falls from the ceiling like feathers floating to the floor.

The people around me are kissing each other as they make promises for the next year. Resolutions they most likely won't keep.

This is my first New Year's alone.

The first not surrounded by my family and friends, instead, sipping on a whiskey neat as I take in the ridiculous joy all around me.

I turn my head to the side, noticing the only couple not kissing in celebration. The woman's back is pressed against the bar, her head angled to the side, with a man crowding her space.

"Come on, sweetie. One kiss. It's New Year's." I hear him say to her.

"No," she snaps, her voice soft but audible above the music. "I don't even know you."

He places his hands on her hips, and she flinches. "Please don't," she begs, squeezing her eyes shut.

The man smiles, but there's nothing friendly about the look. "One kiss," he tells her, not giving up and not giving a fuck either.

I set down my drink on the bar and take a deep breath, hoping I don't end up in jail for the night.

I stalk up behind them. "Hey, darlin'. Sorry I'm late."

Her eyes snap open and widen as I give her a nod, letting her know I know she's not okay.

"Are you bothering *my* girl?" I ask the back of his head.

"Piss off," he snarls, glancing at me out of the corner of his eye.

I cross my arms, squaring my shoulders, and cock my head. "You have two seconds to take your hands off *my* girl, or I'm putting your ass on the ground."

"You with him?" he asks her, ignoring me.

"Yes," she whispers, her eyes still wild.

The man drops his hands from her body, and she ducks underneath his arms. "Hey, sweetie," she says, trying to smile, but her lips quiver. "I've been waiting for you." She places her hand on my chest and plasters her body against my side.

I snake my arm around her shoulders, holding her

closer. “Sorry, I got caught at work.” My gaze swings back to the asshole who’s still staring at us. “You better get—before I make you go,” I tell him, eyes narrowed, lip curled.

He doesn’t move right away, his eyes locked on the woman as he grunts. A second later, he’s gone, vanishing into the crowd.

I tip my head down, looking at her as she clings to my body like a life preserver. “You okay?”

She sags against me, letting out a long breath. “Jesus,” she mutters as her head falls forward, planting her forehead against my chest. “I don’t know how I’m doing.”

I keep my arm around her, still holding her shoulders and not letting my hands drift any lower.

Her body begins to tremble as the adrenaline starts to wear off and the fear settles in.

“He’s gone now,” I reassure her. “You’re safe.”

Her other hand joins the first on my chest before she tips her head back, bringing those big, wild eyes to mine. “I’m sorry,” she whispers.

“For what?” I furrow my brows as I stroke the soft skin near the thin strap of her dress with my thumb.

“I shouldn’t be touching you.” She pushes herself away, grabbing on to the bar to hold herself upright as her body continues to shake from everything that happened.

“I’m pretty sure I touched you first, and don’t be

silly, you needed a rescue, and I was more than happy to give it to you."

Her cheeks turn pink as she tucks a lock of her dark-brown hair behind her ear. "I shouldn't need a rescue."

"We all need a rescue sometime, babe."

"Arlo," she says, glancing at her shoes.

"What?"

She sways a bit but keeps her hand firmly planted on the edge of the bar, holding herself upright. "My name…my name is Arlo, not babe."

"I'm Carmello."

"Hi," she says softly, blinking slowly. "Carmello."

I step forward, placing myself next to her at the bar, and on cue, she turns, resting the front of her body against the counter. "Let me buy you a drink. I think you earned it."

She smiles a genuine smile for the first time since I laid eyes on her. "I owe you a drink."

"Fine. You can buy this round," I lie. "What do you want?"

She leans over, placing her arms on top of the bar, flattening her palms. "Champagne. No, wait." She pauses, her gaze moving across the bottles against the wall. "I need something stronger. Whatever you're having, I'll take."

I nod, motioning toward Jimmy, the bartender and someone I've known since I was a kid. "Two shots of whiskey and two whiskeys neat to sip," I tell him, not bothering to look at Arlo.

"I can't..."

I hold up my hand off to the side. "And two waters."

He nods, making quick work of the drinks as Arlo fidgets at my side. The girl is wound up, but after what she just went through, I'd be wound tight too.

When the drinks are in front of us, I push three glasses in front of her, finally bringing my attention back to her pretty face. "Shot first," I tell her.

"I really shouldn't..."

I lift my shot glass, ticking my chin toward her shot. "It'll take the edge off, and from the looks of you, you need it, darlin'."

"Arlo," she whispers like I forgot.

"I didn't forget."

Her eyebrows rise for a brief moment before she wraps her slender fingers around the glass and brings it toward her lips. The liquid inside sloshes. "I'm shaking," she says, her eyes focused on the drink and the movement I didn't miss.

"I know. It's why you need two. The first one will hit quick, and the second is to enjoy."

Her gaze darts to me and then back to the glass in her hand. She pauses, and I use my free hand to push the shot closer to her lips.

"Down the hatch." I smile before tipping back my shot, swallowing the liquid.

She follows, immediately grimacing and then wincing as the whiskey no doubt burns her insides as it slides toward her belly. "Shit," she hisses, clutching her chest and slamming the empty shot glass back on the bar. "That was…"

"Sip your water."

She blinks, sucking in a breath as if she can't shake the burn. "What?" she whispers.

I push the tall glass of ice water closer to her. "Drink the water. It'll help."

My eyes never leave her face as she wraps her hand around the ice water and lifts it toward her lips, her gaze moving away from me.

"Better?" I ask after her first sip.

She nods with an *uh-huh*, looking everywhere except at me.

"Good." I smile at her again, seeing her shoulders relax even if her eyes are on full alert, moving around the bar area.

She tips her head back, exposing her beautiful neck, before chugging the water like she's at a frat party trying hard to get drunk as fast as humanly possible.

Before the glass touches the bar again, only a few inches of liquid are left.

"You okay?" I ask her again, watching her movements carefully.

Her hands are barely shaking, and although she

doesn't look completely comfortable, she's not as tense or as fidgety.

"Much better," she says. "You can go now, though. I got this," she dismisses me.

"Go?" I raise an eyebrow. "Where am I going?"

She looks over her shoulder at the people still celebrating around us, acting like there isn't a new year every 365 days. "Back to your friends or your girl."

I let out a bitter laugh. "It's just me—and now you."

Her eyes flash for a moment. "How?"

"How what?"

"How are you alone on New Year's Eve?"

I shrug. "I felt like being alone…until now at least."

"But you're…you're," she says and stops.

"I'm what?" I push her.

"You're hot." She rolls her eyes and saves a hand at me. "Like super hot. With your pretty face, perfect nose, high cheek bones, chiseled jaw, and I'm sure you have a six-pack underneath your wrinkles pressed dress shirt."

"Babe, I'm a man who doesn't get manicures, likes to get dirty, and don't need a date or the extra drama just because it's a holiday. And, in case you haven't looked in the mirror lately, you're the one who's super freakishly hot. You're stunning and could get any man in this place or outside of here."

"Well, I…I," her voice dies and she reaches for the whiskey neat, taking a big sip, swallowing down whatever she was going to say in rebuttal. "This has been a long day. I think I need some sleep."

"We're finishing this drink, I'm walking you to your car, and then I'm going home to get some sleep. I'm over this day."

"You don't need to walk me to my car."

"Babe, after what just happened to you, I can't leave without walking you to your car, watching you get inside, and seeing you drive away without that guy getting anywhere near you."

"You really don't need—"

"Don't argue," I tell her, cutting her off. "I'm doing it."

"I can have one of my friends walk me out."

"And where are those friends?" I shift my body, leaning my hip against the bar and turning to face her. "Where were they when *he* had you pinned against this very spot?"

She sucks her pouty bottom lip into her mouth, nibbling on it with her teeth. "Well, they were…" Her voice drifts off, and she looks into the crowd. "They're somewhere around here."

"They're probably shit-faced. I'll walk you out. I won't sleep right unless I know you're safe."

"Why?"

"Why what?"

"Why does it matter to you?" she asks, blinking at me like I've said the craziest shit she's ever heard.

"It's how I was raised, Arlo. You see someone in trouble, you help. You see a woman in trouble, you step in and protect. Until you drive away, I got your back."

She gawks at me again, her eyes searching my face, probably not believing a word I'm saying. "But I'm no one," she says almost flippantly, but there's something about the look in her eyes that makes me feel like she believes that about herself.

I tip my head to the side, furrowing my brows. "Say that again."

"I'm no one," she repeats, but she doesn't look at my face as she speaks. "And I'm most certainly not your problem. I'm sure there are plenty of pretty girls here who'd like your attention."

"Babe," I clip out, pausing for a brief moment until I have her full and undivided attention. "One, don't ever say you're no one. You're someone. Two, I don't give two fucks about all the other pretty girls here. Three, the only beautiful woman I care about is the one standing in front of me. And four, you're not a problem, and even if you were, I could use a problem like you."

Her body stills as I speak, and she clutches her chest, lips parted, blinking. "Well, I…"

"And seeing as you shouldn't drive after you've had too much to drink, we're going to order some fries or maybe a greasy burger, talk for a little while, and then I'll set you on your way."

"But I…"

"Don't like fries?" I raise my eyebrow again.

"Everyone likes fries."

"Everyone?" I ask her.

"Maybe not *everyone*, but those people are monsters."

"Then we'll eat, yeah?"

She tucks a lock of her dark-brown hair behind her ear as the pink hits her cheeks again. "I could eat some fries."

"Burger too. They make the best here."

"They do?" she asks me, telling me she isn't a regular, but I knew that because I would've zeroed in on her if I'd seen her before.

"One bite and you'll never want anything else," I promise her.

"Are you sure you don't have anyone else to be with? I'd hate to keep you from someone."

"Babe, I came alone and planned to leave alone. I just wanted to stop by for a drink, watch all the happy bullshit, and go to bed. I have no plans. No hot date waiting for me. Nothing. Nada. No one."

"Okay," she whispers.

"Fries and a burger?" I ask her again.

She nods with a smile so small I almost miss it.

"Jimmy," I call out as he breezes by us, the bar area busier than it was a few minutes ago. He looks my way, stepping back in front of where we're standing. "Can I get two burgers and fries?"

He grimaces, tipping his head and sucking in a breath between his teeth. "Kitchen's only making fancy shit tonight, man. I can probably twist an arm for a basket or two of fries, but that's about it."

"Fuck," I hiss, my mouth already watering at the thought of a greasy burger. "Two fries will work."

"I'll try my best," he says before disappearing into the back.

"Come here often?" she asks me, her eyes on the swinging door where Jimmy has gone.

"Not *often* often, but I've known Jimmy most of my life."

"Small towns," she sighs, bringing the glass of whiskey to her mouth.

"Seeing as I've never seen your face, I assume you're not from around here."

She shakes her head as she pulls the glass away, licking the liquid from her lips. "Chicago."

"No shit. I have family in Chicago. Great fucking city."

"It's the best," she replies, her lips no longer curved into a smile. "I wish I'd never left."

"Why did you leave?"

She shrugs. "Sometimes life requires a fresh start."

"Ain't that shit the truth," I mumble under my breath.

I've wanted a fresh start for years, putting the nightmare of that night behind me. But I know, no matter where I go, the memories will always find me. There is no escaping the reality, regardless of how far away I put myself.

"Fries will be out in five," Jimmy says, pulling me out of my thoughts.

"Thanks, man."

"Anytime," he tells me before taking off toward the other end of the bar, where some barely dressed girls are using their breasts as a lure to get his attention.

"My knees feel funny," Arlo states before taking another sip of her drink.

I grab on to her arm near the elbow as she starts to sway, and with the other hand, I push the tall stool behind her ass. "Sit."

She plops backward, her ass landing on the edge of the stool, and gapes at me. "You're very…"

"Handsome?"

"No."

"No?"

She smiles, and it lights up the room. "Well, kind of, but that's not the word I was going for."

"I'm wounded."

She tips her head back, laughing, and places her hand on my arm. The contact is innocent, but her touch scorches me. "You're crazy."

"I've been called worse," I tell her, doing nothing to move my arm away from her hand.

"I find that hard to believe. You seem sweet."

"Looks can be deceiving."

"I didn't say you looked sweet." She smirks. "You look like sin, but what you did tonight is sweet."

"I look like sin?" I raise an eyebrow, giving her the smirk right back.

"You look like trouble."

"Got me there, beautiful."

Beautiful is an understatement.

Her green eyes are so striking, I can't stop staring at them, even if they are framed by thick black glasses. My gaze doesn't even wander lower to check out her rack, which is typically where it goes after I see a pretty woman's face.

Jimmy places the basket of fries between us, and Arlo instantly moves her hand away like we've been caught having a moment we shouldn't be having.

"These look great," she says, immediately grabbing a fry, but I touch her wrist, stopping her before she pops it into her mouth.

"Babe. You still want a tongue?"

She looks at me funny before her eyes dip to the French fry hanging between her fingers. "What?"

I tick my chin toward the little potato. "I don't even know how you have skin on your fingers holding that fry, but your mouth won't fare so well."

She drops the fry, the burn finally hitting her skin. "Shit." She places the pads between her lips and slides them into her mouth. “I wasn’t thinking,” she mumbles around her fingers.

“Happens to the best of us. Just give them a minute to cool down.” I nudge her glass of water in front of her. “Hold it.”

“What?” she says, looking at me like I’m a weirdo again, but she’s the one with her fingertips still in her mouth. “Why?”

“The cold glass will stop the burning.”

She shakes her head, muttering under her breath. “Sorry. It’s been a long night.”

“Don’t apologize. How could you know about the wicked ways of their French fries? But now you’ve learned—the hard way, mind you, but you learned.”

She reaches for the glass of water and lets out a loud sigh when her fingertips slide against the cool condensation.

“Better?”

“Much,” she says, leaning forward over the bar, looking more relaxed than she was a few minutes ago. “Thank you.”

I test a fry, giving her fingers a break. “They’re better now, but you may want to blow on them.”

“You go ahead,” she replies, smiling at me again. “I’ll let you test them for safety reasons.”

She watches my hands carefully as I place the fry against my lips before pulling it between my teeth. Her eyes are glued to my mouth, her lips parted, and the air changes, almost crackling around us.

When my tongue sweeps across my bottom lip, taking in the salt, her lips part even more. "Guess they're safe," she whispers.

"They're perfect."

"They sure are," she says, but she's not looking at my eyes or the fries. Her gaze is still firmly planted on my lips in rapt attention.

"You going to have one?" I ask her when she doesn't move.

Her cheeks turn pink. "I should go."

"You don't have to leave."

She glances down at her hand still wrapped around the glass, gripping it like her life depends on the connection. "No, really. I have to go," Arlo says, pushing herself away from the bar, releasing the glass. "It's late, and I've been enough trouble."

"Wait," I tell her, reaching into my pocket to grab some money and at least walk her out. "You can't go out there alone."

"I've been alone my entire life," she says, backing away toward the crowd. "You've done enough."

I barely get a fifty on the bar before she's already a dozen feet away. "Hold up," I call out, trying to be heard over the music, but she turns her back and rushes through the sea of people.

I chase after her, worried about her safety and the creepy guy from earlier. My eyes search the crowd as I head toward the door, knowing exactly where she's headed.

When I make it outside, she's hauling ass across the parking lot, checking to her left and right after each step. She may claim she's used to being alone, but no matter what she says, she's not comfortable with it either.

I stay where I am, feet firmly planted, arms crossed, watching her every step until she stops at a black Mustang, unlocks the doors, and folds herself inside.

And just like that…she's gone.

2

Six Months Later

The sun is setting, kissing the horizon as I blow past a car on the side of the road. I glance in my rearview mirror, catching sight of a woman sitting on the hood, elbows on her knees.

I want to keep going, but I hear my parents' words, telling me never to leave a woman stranded and alone. They drilled into me about doing the right thing even when it puts me out or makes me late. There are worse things they could've instilled in me, but there're still times when the *do-good* ways are a complete pain in my ass.

Victoria, the newest woman offering herself up to me on a silver platter, isn't going to be happy about my being late. We've only been on two dates, and after tonight, I plan to end things with her. I don't want her getting used to me being around or thinking she has a place in my future.

No one has that spot.

There has been a hole there since Carrie died, mingled with guilt, and no matter what I do, I can't seem to bury it.

The road's empty as I swing the bike around, heading back toward the black car and the woman who may not need or want my help.

Her head comes up as I get closer, her brown hair flowing in the soft, humid breeze that does nothing more than blow the hot air around, making it cling to your skin.

She straightens her back, hopping down from the hood, her body going rigid and on high alert. If I could describe someone as a deer in headlights, it would be her.

Rolling to a stop, I cut the engine and remove my helmet. Her eyes meet mine, green and big, emanating fear.

"Need help?" I ask, running my hands through my hair.

"Um," she mutters, blinking. "I don't think so."

I tilt my head, straddling the seat. "You don't think so?" I repeat her words back to her, confused.

"Well, I mean…" She glances down, kicking at the gravel below her shoes. "I think it's overheated. It'll be fine in a few minutes."

There's something familiar about her, but I can't place it. Maybe she's a friend of a friend or someone I've seen around our small town.

"How long have you been out here?"

"A little while," she answers, being evasive.

"I won't hurt you."

"Okay," she whispers, but she's holding her keys in her fist, a move I've seen many women make when taking a defensive stance. "But I'm really fine."

"Want me to take a look?"

She shrugs, barely looking at me, almost hiding her face. "No. I'm okay. You can go."

I sit there, stunned and staring. "I can go?"

"Yeah. You can go. I got this."

"I can't leave if you need help."

"I'm fine," she argues. "I don't need help."

"We all need help sometimes, and I can't leave you out here in this heat all by yourself and just go about my night."

"You can. You totally can. I'll get by. I always do."

"I can't leave you here alone."

"I've been alone my whole life, but I appreciate your checking on me."

Her words strike me as odd. The same words I heard from the pretty girl on New Year's Eve. Words that have never left me, along with the sadness that hung from her lips.

"Do I know you?"

She shakes her head but doesn't look my way, staring down and shielding her face from my view.

"We've met before. Haven't we?"

The woman is beautiful, totally a face I'd never forget, but for the life of me, I can't place her. One thing I know is I never forget a face, especially one as pretty as hers.

She stares at me for a minute, studying my face before her eyes widen again. "Wait. I think... No way. That's so weird," she says, tilting her head, still soaking in the wonderfulness that's me. "I think we met on New Year's Eve."

Ding. Ding. Ding. She *is* her. The woman I met who was pinned against the bar by the sleazy bastard, the one who ran out without even tasting the French fries or waiting for me to walk her to her car.

"Arlo," I whisper.

She blinks. "You remember my name?" she whispers, touching the scoop neck of her tank top, fiddling with the material.

"I do, babe." I smirk, unable to forget it after that night. "You ran out of the bar so fast, I thought your ass was on fire."

Her cheeks turn pink again. "I'm a little awkward sometimes. I don't people well."

"I don't think I people well either."

"You saved my butt that night. I'll always be grateful for that."

"Looks like I'm about to do it again." I climb off the bike and move in her direction. "Now, are you going to tell me what's wrong with the car, or do I have to guess?"

She throws her arm out toward her car. "Front tire is flat, but I can't get it off. I've changed tires before, too many more times than I'd care to admit, but this one won't budge." She starts pacing in front of the car. "I don't know why I can't get it off, but I can't, and I think I'm about to lose my shit. I was just sitting here, trying to figure out my next move, which also included taking a sledgehammer to this piece-of-shit car instead of calling for a tow. But then I couldn't trade it in for a new car, so I scrapped that idea about thirty seconds before you rolled on by."

I stare at her, listening to her ramble on about the car, the tire, her decisions, and honestly, I'm dizzy. The girl had barely spoken to me before and had been cagey as hell since I'd rolled up to her this time, until now, when she decided to verbally shit her entire thought process for the last so many minutes.

"I'll change it."

She crosses her arms, her eyes trained on me. "The rim is bent."

"You bent the rim?" I ask.

She rolls her eyes. "I just said that."

"You don't drive on a flat, babe."

"Babe," she throws back and starts to pace in front

of her Mustang. "I know, but I didn't know it was that bad. And based on where we're standing, I didn't have anywhere to add air in the tire either. I was heading to the gas station when it decided to take a complete shit. I kept driving, and poof—" she throws her arms wildly in the air "—fucked-up rim."

I don't know why, but I can't stop the smile from spreading across my lips. This girl is so weird. She's quiet and shy one minute and totally off the rails the next. She's shy, yet not. Strong, but weak. She's a conundrum wrapped in a pretty package with big eyes, a stunning face, and a smokin' hot body.

"Did you call a tow?" I ask after she pauses long enough to take a breath.

Arlo stops moving and faces me, her lips flat. "Of course I did, but they said it'll be a few hours."

"Cancel them," I tell her, reaching into my pocket to grab my phone.

"What?"

"Cancel. Them."

She gapes at me as I lift the phone to my ear, making the call that I know will get us a fix quicker than her current company.

"Yo." I hear from the other end.

"Mammoth."

"What's up, Mello?"

I stare at Arlo as she continues to watch me, lips parted, eyes carefully studying my every move. "Can you send someone with a tow out to County Line near the Vet about two miles west of the tollway?"

"Sure thing. Give him thirty to get there. You okay?"

"I'm great. My friend Arlo busted a tire and bent the rim. Think you can squeeze her in tomorrow?"

"One of the guys can do it. It'll be done by noon."

"Thanks, man."

"What's Mello want, baby?" Tamara asks Mammoth on the other end of the line.

"His friend's car has a flat," he tells her.

"Oh," she says in a dejected voice.

"What's with the voice?" he asks.

"I was hoping for something a little more…fun."

"Sorry that a guy with a busted tire isn't enough fun for you," Mammoth replies.

"Not a guy," I throw out there, my eyes still on Arlo, studying the lines of her face.

"Oh," comes from Mammoth.

"Oh, what?" Tamara asks.

"Not a man, princess. A chick."

"Mello and all his pussy. You're not doing a free job for one of his random bitches," Tamara says in the background.

"Not one of mine," I say softly, and Arlo's eyebrows rise. I shake my head. "She just needs some help."

"Not one of his," Mammoth repeats.

"Still not doing it for free," Tamara mutters. "His

wife? Yeah. Random chick? No. Piece of ass he's tappin'? No. Fiancée? Sure thing. Get me?"

"Got you, princess," Mammoth whispers.

"He got me?" she asks him.

"I got her," I grumble.

"Got to go, man. Tow will be there soon, and I have a spicy chick to deal with."

"I'm not spicy," she argues.

"Princess, you're not bland," he says with a hint of laughter.

"I'll catch you two later," I say, disconnecting the call before I hear shit I don't want to hear.

"Who's Mammoth?" Arlo asks me, now leaning her ass against the hood of her car.

"My cousin's husband. He owns a body shop. Tow will be here in thirty, and your car will be fixed by noon."

"Noon as in noon tomorrow?" she whispers and lifts her hand to her mouth, biting on her thumbnail.

"Yeah, babe. It's almost dark, so the closest noon is noon tomorrow."

"Shit," she mutters, chewing a little more on that poor nail.

"What's wrong?"

"Nothing," she tells me as she pulls up her legs, going back into the same position I saw her in as I blew past her on my bike. "It's fine."

"What's wrong, Arlo?"

She waves her one hand, still chewing on her other.

I take a step forward, closing the space between us. There's no logical reason why I'm putting in so much effort with a woman who doesn't want the attention, but I can't stop myself.

I've become used to difficult women. I've been surrounded by them since birth.

"Babe. Talk to me."

She doesn't look up or speak, just keeps chewing with her eyes on my boots.

Lifting my hand, I place my fingers under her chin and force her head upward. "Talk."

Her breathing almost stops as she stares up at me with those wild eyes I first saw six months ago. Her hand falls away from her lips, and our gazes lock. "I don't know how I'm going to get home or back to my car tomorrow. I haven't made too many friends since I moved here. At least not any I can call for something like this."

"Well, you got me or Uber."

"I can't Uber," she whispers, her gaze still locked with mine. "They're not safe."

"They're safe, Arlo, but you still got me," I tell her, but I like the idea that she doesn't feel comfortable riding in a car with a random stranger. I'd much rather have her fine ass on the back of my bike, even if it's just for a few rides. She's cute as hell and quirky as shit, reminding me of half the crazy women in my family.

"I'll bring you home and pick you up tomorrow to take you to Mammoth's garage."

"Why?" She blinks.

"Why what?"

She furrows her eyebrows. "Why would you help me?"

"Are you suspicious of everyone?" I ask her, loosening my hold on her chin but still keeping my hand there.

She stays silent.

What would cause someone to be afraid of almost everything? She seems strong, but there's something about her that causes her to pause or see the worst in almost everything.

"Because I'm nice and don't like to see a woman in trouble."

Her response is to stare at me, blinking and confused. "But what do you want out of it? I'm not sleeping with you," she says softly.

Normally, I'd lean forward a little, trying to lure her in, but I don't know this chick—and from the little bit I do, she wouldn't dig it. I'm not the type of man who pushes my way into and onto people, especially not scared little creatures like Arlo.

"If I wanted pussy, I'd go on my way to the one waiting for me. I'm not here to get you into bed, babe. I'm here to help, which is what I'm offering and not my cock."

She blinks a few times, all in rapid succession. "Well, I…"

"So, you want a ride or not?"

She stares at me for a second, her eyes searching mine as I do the same. "Yes," she whispers, and I drop my hand.

"Good. Fuck, you're difficult. Was that really that hard?"

She crosses her arms, guarding herself from me or the entire conversation. "More than you'll ever know."

"Why do you always say you can do shit yourself and you've been alone your entire life?"

She shrugs one shoulder. "Just have."

"You're alone?"

She unfolds her arms, spreading them wide and looking cute as fuck, along with a bit crazy. "See anyone else around here?"

I laugh, shaking my head. "Babe, by your logic, I'm alone too. See anyone around here for me?"

"Well, no, but you had a Mammoth to call."

"I'm sure you have a Mammoth of your own even if they don't have a garage."

"Nope," she clips. "Just me, myself, and I, baby."

I tilt my head, crossing my arms, and stare at her. "You forgetting something or maybe someone?"

She shakes her head. "Nope."

I point at my face. "Me. I'm here."

"You don't count," she tells me before she starts

pacing in front of her Mustang again. "You're a passerby."

"I'm more than a passerby. This is twice I've saved you."

"I don't need saving."

"Fine. I helped," I argue, but damn, she's saucy, a little bitchy, and filled with so much attitude. Her eyes slice to me, and I can't stop a smile from hanging on my lips. "You always this difficult?"

"Are you always this nice?"

"No," I grunt.

"Then, no, I'm not *always* this difficult."

"Doubtful."

"You can go," she dismisses me, wearing a path in the gravel on the side of the road. "I'll be fine. I'm sure you have better shit to do than stand here with me and wait for a tow."

I reach out and snag her arm, halting her movement because the woman needs to stop for half a second. "Babe."

She turns, all forward momentum gone, but doesn't pull away from my grip.

"If I wanted to be anywhere else, I'd be there. I'm not driving away, leaving you out here in the dark to wait for a tow alone. I have nowhere important to be, but if I wanted to be there, I'd be there. And if you meet a man who's willing to drive away, deserting you on the side of the road, then they aren't any man worth knowing. And once the tow comes, I'll give you a ride home, where I know you'll be safe."

She blinks, staring at me again like I'm speaking a foreign language. "You're way too nice. There has to be a catch."

"No catch, babe. Just me. If you knew my family, you'd understand."

"I don't have one of those."

"One of what?"

"A family," she whispers.

"Really?"

She nods. "You're lucky, honey. Count your blessings."

"I do almost every day, but they can be a pain in the ass, too."

"Pain in the ass trumps loneliness any day."

"Finally something I can't argue with you about," I say with a small smile. "Why don't you get your things together so when the tow comes, we can head out and get you home."

"On that?" she asks, ticking her chin to my bike as she moves her eyes over my shoulder, looking like the hunk of metal is going to reach out and bite her.

"Yeah, babe. On that. Never been?"

She shakes her head. "They're incredibly dangerous."

I chuckle. "I'll drive slow, and I guarantee you'll fall in love."

She stares at me again, blinking at me like I'm the weirdest human being in the world. "With you?"

"With the bike, but me too, possibly. There's a whole lot to like about me."

"You're a whole lot of trouble too. Don't need to spend your life surrounded by people and family to know trouble when I see it. And you, mister, are covered in it."

I release her arm, knowing I shouldn't have my hands on her. "Get your shit, babe."

She stares at me for a beat, smiling back at me as I smile at her. "Fine," she mutters without argument. "But I'm still not sleeping with you."

"Not all men are about pussy," I lie, but at least I'm not when it comes to her.

"Oh, okay," she mumbles, not believing me, and rightfully so.

"At least, I'm not right now."

"There's always later," she corrects me.

"Fuck. You're so difficult," I mutter as she stalks toward the driver's side of the car. "Grab your keys too."

My phone vibrates, followed by a message that reads *Be there in five.*

"He's almost here," I tell her as she reaches into the car, gathering her things. "Call and cancel your other tow so this doesn't turn into a clusterfuck."

For once, she doesn't argue. She slides her finger

across her phone screen, taps a few times, and lifts the phone to her ear. She turns her back and starts to pace up and down the side of the car, far enough away that I can't stop her movement. "Um, hi," she says, her voice small and unsure. "I wanted to call to cancel my tow."

I step back toward my bike, resting my ass on the seat, feet crossed at the ankles, waiting

This is the shit I get for being a good person. A beautiful but supremely complicated chick. But unlike the other pains in the ass in my life, she doesn't want anything from me, not even the shit I'm offering.

"Now what?" she asks me.

"We wait," I tell her, crossing my arms as she puts her ass on her hood again, staring back at me.

The next five minutes will no doubt be the longest of my life.

3

ARLO SCREAMED MOST OF THE WAY BACK TO HER place, holding on to me like she'd fall off at any moment.

"Jesus!" she screeches, jumping off the bike before I even have a chance to cut the engine. "Were you trying to kill me?"

Getting her on the bike in the first place was an issue. She'd never ridden, and I promised her I'd go slow and take every precaution to get her home safe.

I did as I promised, too.

I barely went above the speed limit, and I didn't switch lanes unless absolutely necessary.

I haven't driven that slow and careful since my first ride, but I did it for Arlo because she seemed to stress out about everything.

"Babe, I went slow. We could've walked faster."

She clutches her chest, bent over, almost hyperventilating. "I swear I saw my life flash before my eyes."

"Are you always this dramatic?" I ask, smirking at her. She's cute as fuck even if her neurotic level is off the charts.

She glares at me, still holding her chest like she is willing her heart to slow down. "I'm not being dramatic."

"Dramatic and difficult."

"You're a jerk sometimes, even when you're being sweet. It's completely maddening."

"You haven't spent enough time with me to know that, but we could change that, darlin'."

"No. No." She backs away, moving up her driveway. "It's late. I'm tired." Her hand comes to her mouth as she lets out a fake yawn.

"Be back tomorrow before noon for you," I tell her, glancing at her small house with the lush landscaping.

"I'm going to call a taxi."

I swing my eyes back to her. "You ever see any taxis around here?"

She squeezes her eyes shut. "No," she mumbles. "Fucking small towns."

"Just have your cute ass ready to roll."

"That's it?" she asks, staring at me strangely.

"What else would there be?"

"Most guys would ask to come in at least a few times before they leave."

"I'm not most guys, Arlo. I saved you twice, something no one else did, and I'm leaving you at home, knowing you're safe, without wanting anything else in return. Give me your phone."

Her eyes widen. "Why?"

"I want to put my number in it in case you need to call me tomorrow."

"Okay," she whispers, reaching into her purse and retrieving her phone, unlocking it, and then handing it to me.

I dial my number, letting my phone ring once before hanging up and saving myself in her contacts. "Or call me whenever."

"If I order a car service, I'll call you and let you know."

"No, babe. Don't do that. It's a waste of money. I live close, and I want to go to Mammoth's shop with you to pick it up. The number is for any other time you need to call me—for save number three or anything else."

"Oh," she says, her mouth staying in an O after the words finish coming from her lips. "Thanks." She finally smiles. "I appreciate it."

"You're welcome," I tell her, staying right where I am, straddling my bike in her driveway.

She looks over her shoulder at the house and then back to me. "You can go now."

I dip my chin and shake my head. The woman is

bossy and skittish. “I know, but I’m going to wait until you’re inside, and then I’ll hit it.”

She lifts her hand to her lips, chewing on her nail again, staring at me. “Do you want to come in for a drink?”

I raise my eyebrows.

“I really mean a drink, though, and not sex.”

“Wasn’t looking to get laid, babe.”

She drops her hand, and her lips flatten. “Seriously?”

“Seriously,” I tell her. “Never entered my mind.”

Her lips turn down at the sides. “Oh, well…”

“I mean, it entered my mind, but I’m a gentleman. I’m a man, but not a creep. Although I appreciate the offer, I’m going to head home, and I’ll be back tomorrow.”

Her frown disappears, and she stands a little straighter. “You sure?”

“Yeah. See you tomorrow.”

She lifts her hand and waves, her feet still stuck to the same spot.

I lift my chin toward her house. “Go, babe. I told you I’m not leaving until you’re inside, and I’m not leaving until you’re inside.”

“Night,” she says softly.

“Night.”

She moves toward the door, stopping on her front

porch to unlock the door, but before she goes inside, she glances back and smiles.

The woman is drop-dead gorgeous. Devastatingly beautiful, in fact. Her self-confidence is in the toilet, and she reminds me of a scared mouse, thinking everything and everyone is out to get her.

I wave back before firing up the bike but staying put, giving her a chin lift. “Inside!” I yell over the engine.

She rolls her eyes but does as I say, disappearing inside. The lights in the house flip on, and I see her dark silhouette move around the room.

I don’t linger, taking off and heading toward home instead of heading to Victoria’s. There’s no doubt she’d give me attitude for being late, and I’m not about to be bitched out by a woman who isn’t even mine. The pussy isn’t worth it tonight.

I’m in my driveway ten minutes later, and when I reach for my phone in my pocket, there’s a message waiting.

Arlo: Thanks for the save again tonight. Please don’t feel like you need to take me tomorrow. I’ll figure something out. You’ve already done enough.

I shake my head, lifting my eyes toward the dark sky and sighing before shooting her back a message to set her straight.

Me: Babe, last time I’m saying it…stop. I’ll be there at 11:30 to pick you up. End of discussion.

I barely make it to the door before there's a return message.

Arlo: Okay. Okay. I don't know what to say.

Me: You already said enough. We're good.

Arlo: Why are you so nice?

Me: Aren't most people nice?

Arlo: I guess I know the wrong people.

I stare at the screen, wondering if I want to know and if she wants to tell me. It's really none of my business, and unless she's offering the information, I'm not asking.

Me: You do. Night, Arlo. See you tomorrow.

Arlo: Night.

I don't even have a beer in my hand when the messages start rolling in.

Victoria: You're an asshole.

I can't argue with her, and I don't want to. She wants to engage because to Victoria, any attention is good attention. I silence her texts, wanting to leave her in the past instead of letting her invade my future.

Tamara: Mello met a chick.

Gigi: What?

Lily: Whoa. Whoa. Whoa. Who?

Rebel: For real?

Jo: Ooooh. This is going to get good.

I grunt, collapsing into my favorite chair, beer between my legs, watching their nonsense in our group chat fill my screen.

Mammoth: Princess, don't start bullshit where there isn't any bullshit.

Tamara: You fixing her car?

Mammoth: Yes.

Tamara: ...

Me: She's no one to me. She was broken down, and I helped. What was I supposed to do?

Gigi: Hmmm. Solid point.

Lily: True.

Rebel: Is she pretty?

Me: What's that matter?

Jo: That's a yes!

Tamara: It's so a yes.

Me: It's not a yes. I'm asking why it matters.

Gigi: Well, would you help someone who wasn't pretty?

Me: I'd help anyone. Looks don't matter when there's a person in need.

Rebel: Mmm-hmm.

Gigi: You seeing her again?

Me: I'm giving her a ride to the shop tomorrow.

Tamara: I'll make sure I'm in the office tomorrow.

Gigi: I think we should all go.

Me: No. Absolutely not. You guys need to stop. She's a stranger, and I'm never going to see her again.

Rebel: She's ugly, then.

Me: No, she's not, but she's not my type.

Lily: You have a type besides ready, willing, and able?

Pike: Why are you ladies ragging on him for helping someone? If he says he's not going to see her again, he's not going to see her again.

Jett: Does he see any of them again?

Rocco: Good point, Jett.

Me: You're all assholes.

Nick: Birds of a feather.

Me: Listen, she's a nice girl. She's the type to catch feelings, and she doesn't need or want a guy like me in her life.

Tamara: Ding. Ding. Ding. She's hot.

Lily: Yep. 100%.

Gigi: Snap.

Rebel: Mello's never going to settle down.

Rocco: Never say never, babe. Look at me. I've never been happier, but that was because I saw you again.

Rebel: I think a trip to the shop is in order for all of us tomorrow.

Me: Don't you dare.

Gigi: How are you going to stop us?

Me: Someone has to run Inked.

Gigi: Tomorrow's our late day. We don't open until two, so there's plenty of time to go to the shop and make it to Inked to prep.

Me: You're ridiculous.

Gigi: Who's with me?

Lily: I'm in.

Jo: I'll be there.

Tamara: Of course, I'll be there.

Rebel: Count me in.

Me: You all seriously need to get a life.

Gigi: We have one, but it's time for you to get one.

Me: I have a very nice life.

Tamara: You have to settle down at some point.

Me: Says who?

Lily: Says your future children.

I grimace as images of family life flash before my eyes. Someday, I want a family, but that day isn't today.

Me: Not yet. I'm enjoying life too much.

Mammoth: You think you're enjoying life, but there's something better about having that one person to be by your side and then the babies.

Me: Y'all are nuts. I'm going to sleep.

Jo: It's not even ten, buddy. You're old AF but just haven't come to terms with it.

Me: I'm not old, Jo. I'm tired, and obviously tomorrow's going to be a long, long, long day.

Rebel: Night. We're going to stay here and talk about you.

Gigi: Well, duh.

Me: I wouldn't expect anything less.

Jo: You have the girl's name?

Tamara: I can get it off her car's registration.

Me: Stop. Go to bed. Spend time with your men. Do something other than worry about my life.

Rebel: Stop being a shit in the pants. Your bed is calling you, Mello. Night, brother.

Rocco: They aren't going to stop. Might as well ignore them.

Gigi: Night. See you tomorrow.

4

Arlo's waiting in her driveway when I pull in, looking hotter than she has the two previous times I've seen her.

Her hair is pulled up in a tight bun, exposing her long, slender neck. She's wearing a crisp white button-down blouse, exposing just a hint of cleavage. The shirt is tucked into a pair of black pants that end near her ankles, showing off a sexy pair of black stilettos with a few toes peeking out at the end.

"Fuck," I mutter, gripping the steering wheel. When my asshole cousins get a look at her at the shop, they'll be all up my shit.

I'm out of my Challenger before she has a chance to get to her door. "Hey," I say with a smile, trying not to let my eyes travel down to her body. "You look nice today."

She tucks a lock of hair behind her ear, glancing down toward the ground. “Thanks,” she says softly. “I appreciate your doing this for me.”

“I know, babe.” I open the passenger door for her, always being chivalrous like I’ve been taught by both my parents. “Let’s not say it again. Friends do favors for friends.”

She stops at the door and turns her face toward me. “We’re friends now?”

I shrug. “We’re whatever you want to be.”

“Friends works.”

“I think you could use a few more good ones. Yours seem to be shit.”

She smiles at me as she folds herself in, looking like she was made to sit inside my baby. “They’re not the best.”

“I got you,” I tell her, but what the fuck am I doing? I have never been able to maintain a healthy friendship with a woman because it always ends in sex.

Always.

I jog around the back, sliding into the driver’s seat next to Arlo. “Fair warning,” I tell her before I push the *start engine* button. “My cousins may be there.”

The color drains from her face. “A cousin?”

“A lot of cousins. They’re super nosy, but nice. Just be calm and ignore half the shit they say. They’re ridiculous at times. You know how families are.”

"Yeah," she mutters, fumbling with the cuff of her dress shirt.

The ride to the shop is short and quiet. Arlo stares out the window, watching where we're going carefully, but she has very little to say to me.

"Here we are," I announce as we pull into the parking lot, thankful we've arrived and no longer have to sit in awkward silence.

"You don't have to come in with me."

I stare at her, hand on the wheel, confused. "Babe, I don't know what men you hang out with, but a man like me doesn't let a woman walk into an auto body shop alone."

"Why?"

"Because men aren't trustworthy, especially men at places like this."

"But it's your family."

"They're especially not to be trusted," I lie, knowing they're going to be all over her like white on rice.

Her eyes widen. "Really?"

"They're good people, but once you meet them, you'll totally understand."

"Okay," she says, her face relaxing.

"Come on, babe." I open my car door, and she follows, meeting me near the front to walk toward the building together.

As soon as I open the door to the shop, I realize the clusterfuck is far worse than I ever could've imagined.

Every single one of my cousins is there and waiting near the reception area, trying to look incognito and like normal, everyday customers.

Tamara's at the counter, a shit-eating grin on her face. "Good morning, you two cuties," she says in a way-too-cheery voice as her eyes sweep over Arlo, and she comes out from behind the counter to wrap her arms around me. "She's cute." Those words are spoken in my ear.

"We're here for Arlo's car. Did the rim and tire get fixed?"

Tamara pulls away, giving her attention to Arlo. "Hi. I'm Tamara, this jerk's cousin. It's so nice to meet you."

"Umm," Arlo mumbles, looking at me out of the corner of her eye as she stands stiff as a board. "I'm Arlo. It's nice to meet you too."

"She's cute," Gigi says behind me, and I turn just as she lifts a magazine above her face to hide.

"Arlo, these are my cousins," I say, waving my arms around. "Well, half of them, at least."

Arlo's eyes widen again, looking like a poor, trapped animal. "Hi," she squeaks.

I point to each one, calling out their names along with Pike and Jett, who came along for the nosy-ass ride. "Glad to see you all have so much to do today."

"We came to see the renovations to the place. It had nothing to do with you." Lily somehow keeps a straight face as she lies. She's spent way too much time around the other women in the family, given the ease with which those words slide off her tongue. "Ignore our grumpy cousin and his attitude. It's our pleasure to meet you, Arlo."

"Thanks," she whispers, still standing there confused and probably scared too. "You have a lot of cousins."

"We're only half," Gigi adds, rising to her feet. "The other half are a bit younger. We travel in two groups, but none of that matters." She waves her hand, walking closer to us. "We're so happy our cousin was able to rescue you last night. He's always been kind to strangers. It's awful to be broken down in this heat, and no one, especially not someone as pretty as you, should be left out there for long."

"We weren't technically strangers," Arlo says, and I immediately grimace. "We met before but only for a few minutes."

Gigi's eyes swing to me as her shoulder drops and her hand moves to her hip. "Oh, really. Someone left that little nugget out of our conversation."

Oh boy.

I lift my face toward the ceiling, cursing.

"So, Arlo, how did you meet our cousin before?" Tamara asks, moving around the corner toward us.

Arlo looks at me, and I nod. There's nothing to hide now. The cat's out of the bag, and it was innocent, just like this time.

"Both were just by chance," I add before Arlo has a chance to speak.

"It was New Year's Eve, and some jerk was hassling me."

"Aww," Lily coos. "Mello is so sweet."

"It was no big deal," I tell them.

Arlo turns to me with a small smile, her eyes and face soft. "But it was a big deal. I don't know what I would've done if you hadn't walked up to us and chased him away."

"Did you spend the rest of the night together?" Rebel asks, getting way too personal.

"No," Arlo answers. "I had one drink and he waited with me until I calmed down, and then we went our separate ways."

"That's it?" Jo asks. "You both just left?"

I nod. "That's it, until last night."

"Did you stay the night?" Gigi asks.

"No, but it's not any of your business if I did."

"We don't really know each other," Arlo responds.

"Car's ready," Mammoth says, walking into the waiting room and coming to a stop to look around. "Jesus. What the hell is happening in here?"

Tamara shrugs. "Just talking, baby."

"Princess, leave the woman alone. She's a customer just like everyone else. You guys look like a bunch of crazy people. I'm sure you're interrogating her."

"We're not," Tamara says.

"They are," I tell him.

"I'm surprised we've never seen you around here before," Gigi says, fishing for information.

Arlo seems to relax as her posture changes, no longer on the defensive. "I'm new in town. I moved here right at the end of last year, and I don't go out often."

"We need to change that," Rebel says. "You should go out with us sometime."

"Total girls' night," Tamara adds. "We could use some fresh blood."

"I'm sure Arlo has plenty of friends," Pike adds, but I know it's not true from the things she's said before.

"The few I have are so-so," Arlo replies, surprising me. I knew the ones she was with on New Year's Eve ditched her, leaving her vulnerable and alone with the asshole at the bar.

"Well, if you have some free time, we'll invite you the next time we're going out."

"That's really kind of you." Arlo smiles, but I keep my mouth shut. She's an adult, and if she doesn't want to go with them, she'll tell them.

"Are you ladies done chitchatting?" Pike asks, standing from his chair. "I want to get to the shop early and get my station set up for the day."

Gigi frowns. "Fine. We can go," she tells her husband. "It was so nice meeting you, Arlo."

"You too," Arlo says, still smiling.

"Don't be a stranger," Lily says, moving toward the door with Jett.

"Call us later, Tam," Gigi says before heading outside with the others.

"Your family is so sweet," Arlo says softly to me.

"They can be, but they can also be a pain in the ass. Sorry they ambushed you like that."

She laughs. "They were fine. It's nice to see how much they love you and to have so many people care."

"It has its moments."

Tamara clears her throat. "This is nice."

I turn my eyes toward her, narrowing them.

"Anyway, car's done and ready to go," Mammoth says, holding back his laughter.

Arlo moves toward the counter, unsnapping her purse. "How much do I owe?"

"No charge. It's taken care of," he replies.

"No. I can't let you do that."

Mammoth looks at me. "I didn't. He did."

Arlo swings her eyes my way. "You can't pay for my car."

"It's done."

She stalks over to me, getting in my face, but not in an aggressive way. "It's not done," she argues.

"It is."

"Oh boy," Tamara says, giggling. "This should be fun."

"I won't let you pay."

"Already did."

Arlo huffs. "Why?"

"I thought you could use a break, and since I know the owner, I got a helluva deal." I smile.

She gawks at me, her arms down at her sides, blinking away. "That's crazy."

"Listen, Arlo. I don't know if this concept is foreign to you, but sometimes it's nice to do something good for someone. When it's your time, pay it forward."

"I still can't let you pay for my car."

"It's done. End of discussion, babe."

"That always goes over big," Tamara says, watching us with her elbow on the counter, chin in her palm. "Nothing like being shut down."

"I'll pay you back someday."

"You got my number. You know where and how to find me," I tell her.

"Arlo, I need you to fill out some paperwork for our files before you go. Is that okay?"

Arlo nods, giving me another smile before moving toward the front desk and Tamara. "I have to head to work. You two going to be okay?" I ask.

"We're good. Right, Arlo?" Tamara says, watching us carefully.

"I'll be fine. You don't need to stay," Arlo replies. "You've done enough, and the last thing I want is for you to be late too."

"Call me the next time you need a save, babe," I call

out, walking backward toward the door and knowing I am doing the right thing.

Arlo isn't the type of girl you sleep with and walk away from, but all I can offer is a night of pleasure, not a lifetime of happiness.

"Maybe," she says as the door closes and I leave her with Tamara, knowing I'll never see her again.

5

Six Months Later

"I think I'm ready, Lily."

She stares at me funny, tilting her head. "Ready for what?"

"To settle down. To find love. The whole thing. This party bachelor life is getting old and tiring."

Fuck. I have to be crazy. I don't know who's more surprised by the words that came out of my mouth, me or Lily.

"Oh my God! Please let me help you," Lily begs, touching my shoulder. "Please. Please. Please let me help you."

She has always been the sweetest one in the family. She was the most innocent until she hooked up with Jett, the notorious high school playboy who nailed all the tail.

She also gave me the most shit about my whorish ways and made it her personal mission to help me turn my life around.

"I don't think there's any helping at this point. I'm so set in my dumb ways."

"That's not true. We're going to find you love. You deserve it, Mello." She gives my shoulder a quick squeeze.

I place my hand over hers. "I don't think I do, Lily. You're sweet. Maybe too sweet, and you always think the best of people, but not everyone deserves love."

"That's some bullshit. You shut your mouth right now."

I jerk my head back, surprised by the forcefulness of her words. Lily had always been the meek and mild one, but lately, the mouth on her has changed dramatically. "It's shut."

She grabs my hands, holding them on top of my knees. "Look at me."

I turn my head a little because I am looking at her already. "I'm looking."

She gives my fingers a squeeze. "No more easy women. Understand?"

"But they're fun, Lily," I argue, getting a glare from her. The same lethal look all Gallo women perfect before they reach eighteen. "Right. No easy chicks," I mutter.

"You want to find your happily ever after, cousin?"

"I'd like to think there's someone out there for me. But really, let's be honest about this…"

"Go on." Those words are said with a dip of her chin, a move I know she's picked up from our mothers over the years.

"Who's going to love a man like me?"

She blinks, her eyebrows pulling down. "A man like you?"

"A serial fucker."

Her lips twitch, but she bites back her laughter. "You are a fucker. That much is for sure, but—" she moves her stool a little closer until our knees are touching "—that doesn't mean you don't deserve to find happiness. You have a lot of love to give someone."

"I think I have more trouble to give than I do love."

"You're filled with love, Mello. Filled with it." She lets go of one hand, lifting her fingers to my chest and placing her palm over my heart. "It's ready to burst out of you just like it is with every man in this family. We just have to get you to think with this—" she presses her palm harder against my chest "—and not that." She drops her eyes to my crotch for only a second, but she's made her point.

"That part of me has to be into it too, Lily. It's hard to find one without the other. It may not work that way for women, but for me, it does."

She leans back, her hands moving away from me.

"We work the same, dum-dum. But you never get past your lower half, letting it lead the way."

"So, what do I do?"

"First, we have to find you the right girl." She crosses her arms over her chest, cocking her head, and studies me. "Then, you take things slow."

"Slow?"

She nods. "You can't sleep with her right away. I was serious when I told you that before, and you rolled your eyes."

I run my hand down my face and groan against my palm. "Do you know how hard that is?"

She flattens her lips because, obviously, she doesn't care. "You can kiss and stuff, just no going all the way. No more home runs for you, big guy."

"Home runs?" I laugh.

"Yep," she snaps. "No rounding third and sliding into home."

"You're a complete weirdo, Lily."

She smiles. "I'm not a weirdo. I'm normal. Do you want to tell your children someday how you met their mother swinging from a pole or during a threesome?"

I've fucked strippers and been in a threesome—hell, even more people than that at the same time. It makes for an awesome story, but do I want to tell one of my kids that?

Of course not.

I'd come up with some dumb-ass cover to shield

them from our stupidity and sexual prowess, not wanting them to take after their pervy parents.

"Naturally, that's not what I want, babe. Come on now. Give me a little credit."

"You're on the path to making it a reality. For the life of me, I have no idea how you don't have a kid yet."

"Condoms, babe."

"Well, you could be the poster child for their efficacy."

"I love when you use big words," I tease her.

She rolls her eyes again.

"What are you two talking about?" Gigi asks, plopping into the seat next to us.

"Carmello's ready to find love."

I groan and squeeze my eyes shut, swearing under my breath.

"Wait. Hold up. He's what?" Tamara says, joining the conversation.

"He wants to settle down and have a family."

My eyes snap open to three females gawking at me. "No. No. No. I said I was ready to settle down. I didn't say anything about having kids."

The three of them smile in unison, and the regret I feel for telling Lily amplifies.

"Oh. My. God," Tamara says and smacks my leg. "This is the best news ever. Rebel and Jo, get your asses over here."

I stretch out on the lounger, throwing my arm over

my eyes, wishing I could vanish in a cloud of smoke to avoid the conversation they are no doubt going to have at my expense.

Rebel and Jo are next to us a moment later.

"What's going on?" Rebel asks, the two of them casting a shadow over me as I try to enjoy the afternoon sun.

"Mello's ready to start a family," Tamara lies.

"Not what I said," I mutter.

"What?" Jo gasps. "For real?"

"Yes!" Lily screeches, filled with so much glee, I'd even be excited if they weren't talking about me.

Rebel laughs. "Why doesn't he look excited, then?"

"I'm right here. You can ask me," I tell her.

She kicks at my chair. I don't need to see it to know it's her. "Then why aren't you excited?"

I lift my arm, staring up at Rebel as the sun surrounds her with a halo of light. "Because I said I want to settle down, but I never said I was ready to start popping out kids, being tied down to family life filled with no fun."

"We have fun," Gigi argues. "Who here doesn't have fun?"

I turn my head and narrow my eyes. "Your idea of fun and mine are two very different things."

She shakes her head and whispers, "Moron."

"Seriously, though. What's your idea of a good time now that you have a husband and a family?"

"There's no difference except I know who's going to be sleeping next to me every night."

I let out a bitter laugh. "There're lots of differences. Do you sleep in on your days off?"

She purses her lips. "No."

"Kids," I mumble. "I just want to try a relationship. I don't know if I'm ready or able to get married and do the whole one-person thing, but I'm willing to try."

Rebel sits down on the lounger next to my legs, waving her hands for me to scoot over. "The whole one-person thing?" She giggles. "You're an idiot sometimes."

"Only sometimes?" Gigi asks her.

"Mello, babe." Rebel places her hand on my shin, giving it a light squeeze. "You're like your brother in so many ways. Did you ever think he'd settle down and do the one-person thing?"

I stare at her, thinking if I had a woman like Rebel, I'd figure out a way to do the one-person thing just like my brother did. "I didn't for a long time, but I knew once you were back in the picture along with Adaline, he wasn't going to let you go again."

"We just have to find you your person," Jo says, like somehow it's that easy.

"And that would be?" I ask her.

She shrugs. "There's someone out there for everyone."

"Who would be his match?" Lily asks no one in

particular, staring out across the lanai at my grandparents'. "Who could we set him up with?"

"Hmm," Gigi mutters.

"Lemme think," Tamara says.

"You know…" Jo adds.

Lily sits up, placing her bare feet on the cement and looking toward the women who are on the other side of me. "Who?"

"Yeah, Jo. Who?" I ask, curious.

Jo taps her chin and glances upward. "No, I forgot she's knocked up."

"Yeah, let's skip that one."

Rebel smacks me. "Single mothers are very good catches."

"Babe, you were a good catch, but not all single mothers are a good catch. And the last thing I need is to be playing with the emotions of someone who may get attached too quickly. It'll be hard for me to break their heart."

Rebel rolls her eyes. "You're not the heartbreaker you think you are."

I pull myself up to a sitting position. "I never said I was a heartbreaker, but I'd hate myself if I had to break a single mom's heart. I'd rather be with someone who didn't have extra—"

"If you say baggage, I'm going to punch you in that pretty face," Rebel tells me, glaring at me.

Lily pats me on the shoulder. "We'll find you someone. I promise."

"Are you sure you can give up your barfly, whorish ways?" Tamara asks me.

"You gave up yours, didn't you?"

"Oh shit," Gigi gasps and covers her eyes with her hand. "He's looking to die."

Tamara drops a shoulder. "Wanna say that again, cousin?"

"Nope. Not particularly."

"Just leave it to us, and we'll find someone you can't resist. You keep *dating* all the wrong women. It's all about the perfect match," Lily says.

"And that would be?" Jo asks.

"We'll talk about it later when he's not around. It's best if he doesn't hear the conversation," Lily replies.

"I think it's best if I'm here for the conversation," I argue.

"I think we should set you up on a trial run with someone we know can test you and your dedication. We'll get some feedback, and then we can find you your forever person," Lily says, still taking the lead.

"That's stupid," I tell her.

"No, it's not. Just leave it to me. I got you." Lily smiles.

"He needs a freak in the sheets, Lily, not someone who knits for fun," Gigi says.

Lily throws her the middle finger. "Those women

are some of the biggest freaks. Don't judge a book by its cover, babe."

"Oh, okay," Gigi teases. "I'm totally sure they're wildcats in the sack."

Lily crosses her arms and glares at Gigi. "He needs to get to know whoever it is before he sleeps with them. He's always too quick to jump into bed with women. He needs to slow his roll."

"Oh boy," Rebel mutters. "This should be interesting."

"Interesting is never a good thing," I tell her.

Rebel taps my leg again. "Don't worry, brother. We got you. Do you trust us?"

I look around at their hopeful faces. The one thing I know about my crazy-ass cousins is they'll never do me wrong. Even if they think I'm an asshole sometimes, they only want the best for me.

"I do," I say, sealing my fate.

6

THE FRONT DOOR TO THE SHOP OPENS, THE BELL ABOVE it ringing loudly. "Hello?" A woman's voice echoes into the work area. "Lily? You here?" The voice is familiar, but I can't place who it belongs to.

"Yeah, babe," Lily calls back.

"Be right there!" Lily then yells to her, giving me a devilish grin as she leans forward, getting close to my face. "She's here for you. Not me."

My eyes narrow, and I drop my voice low so the girl doesn't overhear us. "What did you just say?"

"She's one of my good friends and wants a tattoo, and the bonus is, you know her too."

I raise my eyebrows and clutch my chest. "Oh. You scared me for a minute. How's that a bonus for me?"

Lily gives me a nervous smile. "Don't get mad, but…"

Nothing good starts with *Don't get mad, but*. Not a goddamn thing. Especially when it comes from the mouth of a Gallo.

"But what?" I ask, folding my arms across my chest.

"She may be here for a little more than a tattoo," she says, her voice rising on the word may.

"Lily," I warn, but I can't find it in my heart to be pissed at my cousin.

"Oh, hush. She's dropping in for a consult today, but I think she's the one for you—or at least someone who can ease you into a relationship or the idea of being in one."

"The one?"

"She's perfect, Mello, and you two had chemistry."

"Had?"

"You met her a few times, but she's been hanging out with us and comes to book club, where we don't always talk about books."

Oh, goodie. A Lily book-club girl. She probably wants a rose on her arm or something like that. It's what most newbies to tattoos always get as their first one.

"She'd better not be someone I've slept with already."

Lily laughs, waving her hand. "Oh God, no. You only met a few times, but she's going to be great at giving me feedback so we can move you in the right direction. We have to work out a few of your chinks first."

"Kinks or chinks?" I ask, waggling my eyebrows, trying to find humor in a situation where there is none.

"Your issues," she explains, sucking the fun right out of the possibilities.

But then again, how much fun could I have with a bookish chick? Probably not much since I don't enjoy sniffing books and discussing the easter eggs an author drops in as clues.

"I don't have issues when it comes to the ladies."

"Uh, yeah, you do when it comes to commitment. And she's going to help me help you learn how to slow things down." Lily turns her head toward the front of the shop. "One more minute, sweetie," she calls out before turning back to me.

"No rush. I'm sitting here finishing my book. One minute, one hour, it's all good."

Fucking fabulous.

She carries books with her, and time doesn't seem to matter to her when she's licking her finger, swiping the pages. Sounds like a rip-roaring good time.

I roll my tongue piercing between my teeth and over my lip, trying to stop myself from raising my voice. "Are you fucking serious with this?"

"Totally." She nods, a huge smile on her face, looking like she does at Christmas. "I've put a lot of thought into this. I can't fix you unless I know what's broken, and she's perfect for this." She stands but doesn't leave, just claps her hands together like she's about to open the Christmas present she's been dying to get her hands on. "She's like the romance whisperer, and since you two know each other…she was my first choice."

I peer up, trying not to look at her like she's a total weirdo goofball, but she so is. "Why is she perfect, Lily?"

"Well," she says, biting her lip like she knows a secret I don't. "Because she's drop-dead gorgeous."

"Debatable and subjective," I mutter.

"She used to be a model."

"Then she's not that pretty if she used to be." I cringe when I say those words because I'm being a dick.

Lily leans over, hands on her hips, sticking her face right in mine. "No, jagoff. She used to model full time but got sick of all the travel. She is literally going to make you drool."

"Okay," I snort, but my gaze moves toward the front of the shop, where there's only a single red shoe tip visible. "Why else? 'Cause I've fucked beautiful girls before, babe."

She clicks her tongue, chuckling. "You're not going to fuck her, Mello."

"Hot chicks dig me. Hell, *all* chicks dig me. I'll have her under me in a day."

"She's a virgin," Lily blurts out.

It's like a slap in the face and a challenge at the same time. My eyes widen, my heart beats a little faster, and my dick gets completely hard. "She's a what?" I whisper, swallowing my tongue because this could be bad, really bad—or maybe good, so, so very good. "You're shitting me."

"I'm not shitting you." She cocks her head, giving me a small laugh. "So, no matter how hard you try, you're not getting in her pants. But she's promised me to take great notes. Think of her as your teacher for the next month."

"You *are* totally shitting me." Jesus-fucking-Christ, this is going from bad to worse, sounding more like school than a good time. "And what the hell with taking notes?"

Lily nods again, her smile only widening. "Yep. We're going to nail down your issues and fix them so you can find your HEA."

"My HEA?"

"Your happily ever after."

I roll my eyes this time. "One, I'm not broken, babe. Two, fake dates aren't going to work because I won't act like me, so her notes will be worthless. And three, what's going to make me even want to try if there's no chance of getting laid in any way?"

Lily taps her chin, but the curve to her lips doesn't go away. "One look at her and you'll chase that tail, no matter where she goes or what she gives. You're going to try harder than you've ever tried before, Carmello Caldo. Of this, I have no doubt."

"You're getting me excited here, Lil. I need a moment before I can walk out there and see her," I tease, giving my little cousin a wink.

She groans a slew of curse words under her breath. "You seriously have a problem."

"I do not. Ask the women I've been with. No problems for me, love. And I'm totally fucking with you. I don't walk around with my dick hard all the time."

"Thank God," she mutters.

"Only sometimes. I'm a man, Lil. My body just does shit I can't control."

"Up," she demands, motioning for me to rise. "It's time to get ready to meet your teacher for the next month."

"Ooh, is she going to paddle me?" I ask as I stand. "I've been a bad, bad boy."

Lily purses her lips. "You're going to be a tough nut to crack."

"Literally," I whisper.

"It's just a short time, Mello. And afterward, we'll have you on the road to your greatest desire and one step closer to a family."

"After a month, my greatest desire will be an orgasm."

Lily rolls her eyes again until the blue disappears.

Then it hits me.

Duh.

There's always a loophole.

"Wait, I can see other people, though, right?"

"You want to date?" she asks.

"Well, no, but I'd like to bang some chicks, or I'll seriously have blue balls after a month of nothing."

Lily grabs my wrist, raising it between us. "You have a hand, darling. You'll get used to using it."

"My hand?" I gawk at her. "I'm not ten."

"Ten?" she whispers, her lip curling in disgust. "You were masturbating at ten?"

I shrug, pulling my hand away. "Maybe nine. I don't remember, but I didn't have hair on my balls yet."

She pretends to gag, but I ignore her. "Boys are so gross."

"So, sex with other chicks…a yes or a no?"

"Do you really want your forever?"

I think on it.

Sex or forever?

Sex or forever?

God, that is a damn hard choice.

I am a man accustomed to pleasure and haven't gone without sex for an entire month since my voice changed.

Could I do it? That is debatable.

But when I glance at Lily, she looks so hopeful and excited, I don't have it in me to kill all her happiness and the dreams she has for me.

I place a hand on each of her shoulders and stare her straight in the eye, promising something I never thought I'd promise. "I won't sleep with anyone else, Lily. You have my word. I'll only fake date. If someone's going to give me an orgasm, it'll be her or my trusty left hand."

"But you're right-handed," she tells me, like that means something.

"I jerk with my left."

Her head lurches forward, and she covers her mouth. "I can't. This is too much." After a few seconds, she finally stops pretend puking. "She's really going to have her work cut out for her, and the notes are going to be long. Probably a novel by the end."

"I'm going to give her the full Carmello treatment."

"Oh God," she whispers, her eyes wide.

I smile, knowing I got this shit won even if it's not a contest. "She's in good hands. I promise."

Lily shrugs off my hands, squares her shoulders, and says, "No, Mello. You've got it wrong, baby. I'm not worried about her. It's you I'm worried about. I don't think you're ready for what's going to happen."

"I'm not scared, Lil. Bring it," I tell her, welcoming the challenge.

Lily looks at me one last time before going to greet Arlo the front of the shop. "Prepare yourself."

"Totally prepared," I mutter. "I'll meet you out there in a few. I need a moment."

"Don't take long," Lily says, giving my shoulder a light squeeze. "Or your future may leave before it starts."

7

"What are you doing?" Those words come from Gigi as she walks through the back door of the shop, finding me leaning over my station, talking to myself while Lily talks to Arlo.

"Praying."

The clicking of her high-heel boots stops a few feet away, and I lift my head to look at her, knowing what I'm going to see. "You're what?" she asks with her nose wrinkled and eyes trained on me.

"You heard me."

"Well, yeah. But why?"

I turn my entire body around, placing my ass against the cabinet, and cross my arms. "Did you know Lily's setting me up with someone today?" I raise an eyebrow.

Gigi's eyes widen. "Um…" she mumbles.

"Thought so."

"Well…I…"

I lift a hand to her. "Save it."

The women in this family are thick as thieves. I have no doubt Gigi is in on Lily's grand plan, along with Tamara, Rebel, and Jo too. Besides being nosy and unable to keep a secret, they have a constant need to try to fix people. And this month's current target is me.

"You're now part of the enemy camp," I tell her as she stands there, blinking at me, knowing she's been caught and I'm not overly happy.

"Aren't you the one who asked for our help?" she asks me, mindlessly rubbing the back of her neck.

I tick my head toward the front of the shop. "Yeah, but I thought I'd get some warning, not have her show up at work as a surprise."

Gigi gasps. "She's here? Like, here, as in now, now."

"That's what I said."

"Lily didn't tell me she was stopping by today."

"She's my first appointment. She's more than stopping by, but at least it's only a consultation."

Gigi's eyes widen. "Hold up. She's getting a tattoo?"

"Yep, and I'm the lucky one doing it."

"I know you'll do a great job. But seriously, she's getting a tattoo?"

"Again, yes. What's the big deal?"

Gigi's eyes move around, not meeting mine. "She just never seemed like the tattoo type."

I narrow my eyes, knowing someone's playing me or both of them are. "Listen, it doesn't matter if she's the tattoo type or not. I know why she's here. Lily explained to me the grand plan to identify and fix my issues. I told her I'm game because I've never been scared of a challenge."

"If you're up for the challenge, why are you back here and not up there, welcoming her to the shop?"

Pike strolls in behind my cousin, his wife. He looks at me and then at her. "What did I miss?"

"The woman Lily is fixing Carmello up with is here," Gigi whispers.

"Oh boy," he mutters.

I throw up my hands, glaring at him. "You too? I mean, I expect this shit from the girls. But you, Pike, I thought you'd have my back in shit like this."

He shrugs. "I have Gigi's back first since she's my girl."

"You're a traitor to all dick-kind."

He stares at me, blinking. "Dick-kind."

"The bro code. You're a traitor. Card revoked."

Pike turns his head to where Lily and the girl are talking but still not visible. "Have you seen her yet?"

"Nope."

He stalks toward me, arm out, and pokes me straight in the chest. "Then withhold your judgment, brother."

"Hello," Gigi says, waving her hands. "I'm right here, and I can hear you."

He glances at her, smiling. “Babe, you’re the most beautiful creature I’ve ever met. I’m just calling a spade a spade. You going to tell him she isn’t beautiful?”

“No,” she groans. “I just don’t like hearing you think she’s beautiful. But I ain’t gonna lie, if I were even remotely interested in pussy, I’d be following her around like a puppy dog and totally go lesbo.”

Pike stares at his wife, speechless for a second before he recovers. “You’d leave me for her?”

She comes up behind him, wrapping her arms around his middle. “If chicks were my thing, you wouldn’t be here, sweetie. So, no, I’m not leaving you for her. Anyway, she’s Carmello’s girl.”

“She’s not my girl,” I argue. “She’s my fake girl for a month, and that’s it.”

Pike pulls Gigi around his body, throwing his arm over her shoulder, both fuckers laughing. “He’s so gone and doesn’t even know it.”

“I know,” she says, almost too giddy. “It’s going to be fun to watch.”

“There’s nothing to watch. It’s like the world’s longest homework assignment, or therapy session, by someone who isn’t qualified to diagnose me when there’s nothing broken.”

Gigi’s smile brightens. “Oh, honey. Pike’s right.”

“I’m pretty sure I’m going to break her.”

She stares at me before bursting into laughter. “She can’t be broken.”

"She's never met me. Not the real me, anyway," I tell her, touching my chest, knowing my abilities and how easily I've charmed members of the opposite sex.

"This is going to be the most entertaining thing to watch," Gigi replies.

"Mello!" Lily yells from the front of the shop. "Come here."

Gigi's eyebrows rise, and her smile gets even bigger. "And so it begins."

I tip my head back, staring up at the ceiling, and say another prayer.

"What the fuck are you praying about again?"

"That she's ugly as sin or has bad breath. Something that's going to make this the easiest month of my life."

Gigi chuckles, shaking her head. "You're shit out of luck, buddy."

"Fuck," I hiss, moving away from my station and heading toward Lily and the mystery woman. "I hate you all."

"Good luck," Gigi calls out, teasing me. "Love you."

I give her a middle finger over my shoulder, not bothering to look back at her because she's loving this shit as much as Lily.

The girl's back is to me as I step into the customer waiting area, so all I see is long brown hair, long thin legs, and nothing in particular that makes her so freaking special.

But then she turns around.

"Mello, you two have already met, but just in case you forgot, this is…"

The world slows down the moment our eyes collide.

"Arlo?" I whisper, feeling like someone gut punched me.

"Hey, Mello," Arlo says, her voice sweet and seductive. She lifts one hand, brushing her long dark hair over one shoulder in the sexiest way. "It's great to see you again."

Her voice wraps around me, making it hard to breathe.

This isn't good.

Not good at all.

Get your shit together, man.

She's only a woman. An extremely hot woman, but still a woman. One I am never going to sleep with. I am an experiment to her and my cousin. A pet project… nothing more.

"It's been a while. I didn't know you became friends with my cousin."

"We've been hanging out."

"We've all been hanging out," Lily adds. "We go out every few weeks for 'book club.'"

"No one told me that," I whisper.

"You were on a need-to-know basis, and you didn't need to know. It's not like you were going to come to book club," Lily says.

"I may have," I lie, but I stare at Arlo, soaking in her beautiful eyes and dark hair. She's just as stunning as she was the last time I saw her.

"Lily said you were the best tattoo artist at the shop, and since she wanted me to work with you on the other thing, I figured I'd get a tattoo in the process."

"Ah, right. The other thing. I'm going to warn you now. I love a good challenge."

"Me too." Her smile morphs into a smirk. "But this is more of a learning opportunity than a challenge. I'm not here to push your boundaries."

"Push or cross any boundaries you want, sweetheart. I'm yours for a month."

"It's going to be fun," she says, and I have no doubt it will be. "I needed a project and a little excitement, and when Lily told me about your issue, I thought I could help. You saved me twice, and now it's my turn to return the favor."

"I have no issues," I tell Arlo, but I'm staring at my cousin when I speak. "Not wanting to settle down is not a disease or a weakness. It's a lifestyle choice and not something that needs to be fixed."

"Sure, Carmello. I'm not here to fix you. I'm just a keen observer. But today, it's all about my tattoo consult and laying the groundwork for the next month."

My eyes finally wander, taking her all in, and goddamn, do I love every bit of her. "Where do you want to get the tattoo?" I ask, going back into business mode.

She runs her hand down under her breast to the top of her hip over her ribs. "Right here."

Naturally, she wants it on a part of her body where I have to navigate around her breasts and tons of exposed skin. Of course, she couldn't pick the top of her foot or her wrist to keep shit easy and basic.

"What do you want…a flower?" I ask, knowing she totally looks like she'd have something beautiful and delicate like a flower.

"A dragon," she says softly.

I blink. "A dragon?" I ask, thinking I heard her wrong.

"Yes, a dragon. Why are you surprised?"

"It's just… Do you have a design idea?" I ask her, Lily's head swiveling between as we go back and forth.

"I do."

I fucking hate doing other people's designs, but I'm not one to turn down a job, especially when it's a friend of a family member, even when she's here to fix me.

"I showed her your book, Mello. She wants the dragon on page five."

I swing my gaze to my cousin. "You showed her my book?"

She nods, her brown hair moving as she smiles. "She wanted to see your work, and she fell instantly in love with that design."

"You want *my* dragon?" I ask Arlo this time. "It's not girlie at all, and it's pretty big."

"I'm not super girlie, and I like them big," she says, smiling at me with those green eyes and pretty face. She knows exactly what she said and how she said it, fully aware of how I'd react.

I cough, almost choking on my own spit. "It's a good four hours of work and a lot of pain. It may require more than one session, Arlo."

"I don't mind pain, Mello. I can handle it if you can," she challenges, her eyes sparkling.

"Fuck," I whisper to myself.

This girl is trouble and completely different from the meek and mild woman I met for the first time over a year ago.

And I'm not talking about a little bit of trouble, but a ton of it. How am I supposed to spend a month with her and not have sex?

My fucking ass, she's a virgin.

"If you think you can handle it, I know I can," I tell her, holding my shit together. "I'll get the consultation room ready, and we can go over a few things and come up with a final size and do any design changes. It'll be better to have some privacy."

I don't even have to turn around to know Gigi, Pike, Trace, and Rocco are behind me, elbowing one another, all in on the bullshit. This wasn't just Lily's doing. This was a relationship intervention, and they were all cock-blocking me.

"Whatever works for you. I don't mind being in public," Arlo replies.

"I mind," I say, shocking myself a little. "You're going to have to remove your shirt, and there are going to be a lot of people in and out of here in the next few hours."

"They're just breasts," Arlo says like I'm totally overreacting.

Again. The signs are there.

She is not a virgin.

No freaking way.

No woman who hasn't given herself to anyone would say *They're just breasts*.

Nope.

I'm not believing it.

They're totally yanking my chain and lying to me.

But that's fine.

I can play the game.

"I'm just going to throw this out there, and you can totally tell me to fuck off, Arlo, but this is a big tattoo for your first. You may want to think about something smaller and in a different area."

She steps forward, getting in my personal space, and I do nothing to move away. "Carmello, a woman knows what she wants, and I want it. I want it bad. As for the pain, I can handle it. My pain threshold is really high, and sometimes, I actually enjoy it."

Someone could punch me in the face right now and I wouldn't flinch or feel it. Her words have smacked me down, making my cock hard, and left me winded already.

Arlo is an enigma. Someone I want to peel the layers away from to expose the real woman underneath. So much about her doesn't add up, and I am going to make it my personal mission to figure her out.

"Whatever you want, babe," I tell her. "You want it, I'll give it to you. You want to start the tat today, I have some time this morning and can squeeze you in."

Arlo stares at me and I stare back.

There's a spark and sizzle to the verbal tango we're doing. She likes me, and not in the platonic way either. The chick wants a piece of me, and I will be more than happy to oblige.

"Um," Lily mutters. "Hello…"

"What, Lil?" I ask, but I don't dare tear my gaze away from the green-eyed temptress.

Lily clears her throat and steps next to us to stand to our side. "Maybe you two should move to the other room. We have customers coming in, and your back-and-forth is…"

"Hot," Gigi finishes from behind me. "So fuckin' hot."

"Shall we?" I say, motioning toward the back of the

shop with one hand. "You can keep me company while I prepare everything instead of waiting out here. I'm sure you can read in a quiet room just as easily as you can out here."

She lifts her book to her chest, cradling it against her shirt. "Whatever you want."

She smiles, and my belly flutters like I'm some pansy-ass chick.

I don't really want her reading. I want her on her knees, sucking my cock, but I don't dare tell her. At least, not in front of everyone. I'd save that for a later time once I peeled away a few layers and we are better acquainted. I have no doubt she'd drop and suck me dry, and I'd let her even if it was the end of me.

"You two kids have fun," Lily calls out as I stalk toward the back, my cousins and brothers parting like the Red Sea as we walk through the public work area.

"Nice," Trace mutters, and I know he's checking her out. But I ignore him and keep on walking.

If this chick wants to try to fix me, I will let her do whatever she wants and happily play along with the charade. If she is going to pretend to be my girlfriend, I am going to have as much fun as possible.

8

"DUDE," TRACE SAYS AS I STALK BY HIM, DOUBLE-checking my design while Arlo waits for me in the other room. "She's fucking mint."

"Shut up, man." I collapse into a chair, knowing I'm about to get an earful of shit from my family.

"If you feel too much pressure doing her tattoo or anything else, I'll happily step in and take control of the situation," is Trace's reply.

I snap my head to the side and glare at him. "You better keep your ass in that chair. And get the words *doing her* out of your mouth when talking about Arlo."

He lifts his hands, throwing himself back in his chair. "Someone's touchy," he teases. "She already got your dick all twisted, and it's been what—" he looks at his wrist, then smiles when he looks back at me "—ten minutes."

"This isn't your game to play, li'l man," I announce, setting the ground rules before my little brother tries to make a move. "You need to let the adults handle the situation."

"This is going to be extremely delicious," Gigi adds as she readies her station for her first client. "Super tasty to watch."

"Don't you start," Pike tells her, getting a glare from his wife, but that doesn't stop him. "Leave the man alone. He's going through something, and he doesn't need you guys adding to it."

Gigi turns around, hand on her hip, leveling her gaze at him. "What the fuck is he going through? I mean, besides pussy like it's in limited supply and he's trying to have a monopoly."

"I'm not that bad," I say, earning a laugh from everyone, including my know-it-all cousin Gigi.

"You're clearly out of touch with what you've been doing."

"I'm a man with an appetite, and I'm single. I'm not going to make excuses or apologize for my behavior."

She slides her chair over to me, leaning into my space, eyeing my design like she gives a fuck. "So, what's your endgame with Arlo? Steal her virginity and run? She's too nice of a girl for you to dirty her."

"Nah, Gigi. I know Arlo's sweet. I've met her before —twice, in fact—and she's Lily's friend, so I plan to play by the rules and be a complete gentleman."

She stares at me, studying my face, but I don't dare look at her. I'm not being entirely truthful, and Gigi is a human lie detector. "We'll see," she whispers. "And by the way, she's all of our friend."

"Why didn't you guys tell me you were hanging out with her?" I ask, glaring at my cousin.

She crosses her arms. "Why would we?"

I shrug. "I don't know. I'm the one who found her and introduced her to Tamara and all of you, in fact."

"We didn't see a reason to tell you. She's a good girl, Mello, and while we love you, we didn't want to see her get hurt."

"But now, it's okay?"

"Now, it's different. It's fake, but so help me God, if you..."

"I'll behave, Gigi. I can take a month out of my life to placate my cousin and her whims. Plus, I really do want to move toward something more stable."

Gigi steps closer until I can feel her breath hitting the back of my neck. "So, you're not attracted to Arlo?"

"I didn't say that," I mutter, tweaking the claws of the dragon to make sure they're absolutely perfect.

"Don't use her and then discard her, breaking her heart into a million little pieces like you've done to every other woman you've tempted into your bed."

Her words hit me, cutting a little too close to the quick. "You make me sound horrible."

"You're an unapologetic player, Mello. You never

make promises, but the girls go stupid around you. And while Arlo is one of the smartest and savviest women I've ever met in my life, I also know you have the ability to destroy her."

I finally turn my face, looking straight at my cousin. "Maybe she'll destroy me. Ever think of that?"

Gigi studies me for a second, and then she rolls her eyes. "You'd need to have a heart for that to happen."

"I'm out," I announce, pushing back and out of my chair. "I got shit to do. You guys can stay out here, talking about me and my shitty behavior the rest of the day, but let's not forget, you all were every bit like me before you found your other half."

"I don't count," Trace adds. "You're my pussy hero, and I'm still single."

"Fuck you," I tell him, pointing my finger at him as I stalk by. "You'll never be as great as me."

He laughs, throwing a pen at me and hitting me in the middle of the back. "Go get her, bro," he says.

"He'll lock it down within two weeks," Pike says, getting my middle finger high in the air with my back to him and the rest of the jerk-offs I call family.

I knock lightly. "Arlo, you ready?"

"Yeah, Mello. Come on in," she says, her voice soft and sweet.

I turn the knob, not one bit prepared for what I see when the door opens. I stop dead with one foot inside and everything else still in the hallway.

Arlo's sitting on top of my table, perched with her back against the wall, holding her book, and wearing only a lacy black bra, leaving very little to the imagination.

She looks like a Greek goddess with her dark hair, olive skin, piercing green eyes, and long legs stretched out across my table.

Any other time, any other girl, and I'd totally be putting the moves on her, probably taking her back to my place for a one-and-done.

She peers up, pushing her black-rimmed glasses up her nose, and smiles at me.

Swear to Christ, my heart stopped along with the entire world. I've never seen a girl wearing glasses look so sexy before, and it's doing all kinds of wicked shit to my body and is totally fucking with my mind.

"Hey," she says, her eyes raking over me and not just my face.

"Ready?" I walk in, trying not to stare at her tits, which is super hard because they're fucking fantastic. "You can totally change your mind, and I won't think any differently of you. This is a big commitment. There's no turning back on a piece like this."

She sets her book on top of her legs, giving me a full view of her upper body. It's like a one-two punch to the face, but somehow, I don't swallow my own tongue or start to drool. "It's nice to see you again and not when you need to save me," she says.

“Yeah.”

“I never got to thank you enough for helping me out.”

“There’s no need to thank me, Arlo. How have you been? You seemed—”

“I’m great,” she says, not letting me finish my statement. “I was in a bad place back then, but I’m so much better now.”

“We all have shitty times in our lives, but I’m glad you’re doing better. You deserve to have better.”

“You too, Mello,” she says with a small smile. “That’s why I told Lily I wanted to help when she said you wanted to find your forever.”

“Well, I appreciate your input. I swear I’m not broken.”

“Never thought you were. A guy who’s broken wouldn’t have stopped to help me twice and been nothing but a great guy about it.”

I clear my throat, feeling uncomfortable with the conversation. “You sure you want to do this?” My gaze dips to her exposed ribs and her perfect, blemish-free skin. “We can still fake date without the pain and permanent reminder of me etched on your skin.”

“I want this,” she tells me, never breaking eye contact. “I’ve wanted a dragon for as long as I can remember, and when I saw your drawing, I knew it was the one.”

“I can make it smaller, less intricate, and put it somewhere a little less painful.”

“I want it just like it is,” she says, her eyes dipping to the piece of paper I set next to her when I entered the room. “It’s beautiful.”

“I have something similar. Almost everyone in the family has a dragon somewhere on their skin too.”

“Where’s yours?” she asks, her eyes moving over my skin, searching for the ink.

“On my ribs.”

“Let me see it,” she whispers.

Reaching back, I yank my T-shirt over my head. Her eyes light up, moving over my skin like she’s studying a work of art.

“Turn,” she says, finally letting go of my arm. “Show me all your ink.”

Without hesitation, I stand so my back is at her eye level and turn to face the door. I jump when her warm fingers touch my skin and start tracing the outline of the tattoo on my back I had my brother put there five years ago.

“It’s all stunning,” she whispers, the leather under her body squeaking before her warm breath joins her fingertips as I turn. “The work is exquisite. The dragon is powerful and a slight variation on the one you’re putting on me.”

“I drew them both,” I tell her, my voice strained because I like the way her fingers feel against my flesh.

I close my eyes, letting her get her fill and loving every second her skin is on mine.

"I want it," she says, her fingers moving over my ribs and down the tail of the dragon. "Seeing it in person…the power, the beauty… I know I want it, Mello."

"Whatever you want, babe. I'll give it to you," I say, worrying I mean those words about more than a simple tattoo.

"Good," she tells me, and a second later, the warmth of her fingers vanishes. "I'm ready."

I lift my arms, about to put my shirt back on, when she whispers, "Don't."

I turn, staring down at her. "You want me shirtless?"

"It's only fair," she says with a smile, tipping her head downward to her lace-covered breasts. "Don't you think?"

"You're playing dirty, Arlo."

"Who said I had to play fair?"

I swallow the groan that's hanging in the back of my throat, trying not to fall for her games. "Stand up for me so we can place it right," I tell her softly, knowing the next few hours are going to be more painful for me than her.

She stands, her breasts in my face, arms at her sides. "Like this?" she asks, looking down at me so innocently, I almost fall for it.

"Just like that. I'm going to run my hand across your

skin to see if we need to shave any hair and then place the tattoo. I swear to God, I'm not touching you for no reason."

She laughs, and it's the sweetest sound in the world. "It's okay. Lily explained it all to me. It's pretty hard to tattoo me without touching."

I lift my hand as she stares down at me, and before I can touch her ribs, she places her hands on my shoulders. We're entering dangerous territory and alarm bells are going off in my head, but I don't stop. I can't stop.

I am a professional after all. I've tatted just about every single body part you can imagine. But this is the first time touching a client feels like something else… something more.

Her skin is like silk underneath my palm, smooth and hairless. "Babe," I say, my voice coming out way deeper and betraying the shit she's doing to my insides. "I need you to put your hands down to place the tattoo."

"Sorry," she says, but she's slow to move her hands.

"Stand up straight."

She does, but I can't resist the urge to touch her hips, making sure she's fully facing me. "Don't move."

Arlo barely breathes as I prep the spot, carefully laying the stencil on her skin and rubbing over it with my palms, transferring it to her body.

This simple act of placing her outline may be the most erotic moment of my life, and there's not even any sex involved.

How fucked up is that?

Super fucked up and more than I can wrap my brain around.

If I think about it too much, I'm going to mess this all up, and the last thing I want is to give her a shitty tattoo that'll be the only blemish on her otherwise perfect body.

As soon as the paper is off, she steps up to the full-length mirror on the back of the door. "What do you think?" she asks me, turning from side to side to see it from different angles.

"Beautiful," I whisper, but I'm talking about her and not just my outline on her skin.

"I love it," she says, running her fingers around the outside edges.

I can't stop myself from staring at her in the mirror. Fuck, this is going to be a miserable month.

"You ready?"

"Yeah." She turns toward me, the real thing more spectacular than the reflection. "Promise you'll be gentle with me."

"I promise," I tell her, meaning every word. "Tell me when it becomes too much, and I'll do whatever I can to make you more comfortable."

She climbs up on the table, lying back with her ribs facing me. "You have some music or something? It's too quiet in here."

"What do you want to listen to?" I brace myself,

waiting for her to say Shawn Mendes or some other fluffy-ass girl shit.

"Drowning Pool or something like that would be great."

My eyebrows rise, moving on their own and out of complete shock. "Metal?"

"Hell yeah. Something hard and heavy."

It's official. I'm fucked. Not a little fucked. But totally and completely fucked. It's like Lily gave Arlo the playbook to get to me as fast as possible, plucking my dream girl out of thin air.

I make quick work of it, putting on a metal playlist I've saved and listened to a hundred times.

Arlo stares up at the ceiling, one arm over her head and the other down at her side so I can get full access and see everything too.

I put on my gloves with my eyes trained on her skin. Everything else is ready to roll, but there's a knot in my stomach, something I can't quite place as I pick up the gun. "Small line at first so you can see how it feels."

"Okay," she whispers and holds her breath.

"Make sure you breathe. It's important. I don't need you passing out on me." She doesn't even flinch as I touch her skin.

"Yes, Mello. I'll breathe, but I may need you to remind me every once in a while."

"I'll remind you, babe. I got you."

She turns her face toward me and smiles. "I know you do."

When the needle touches her skin, she squeezes her eyes shut and stops breathing. "You sure about this?" I ask her one final time, because a line, I could make into something pretty and quick, but anything more and there will be no turning back.

"Yes," she whispers, keeping her eyes closed. "I want this. Stop asking and get to it."

"You got it." I go straight into work mode. Ignoring that she's a pretty girl and one I'm going to fake date for the next month.

I am here to do a job, and she deserves my best damn work.

But three hours in, she starts to squirm more than she has before, and I've given her a break every hour. "Let's finish this tomorrow."

"No," she says, those green eyes meeting mine. "I can do this, and I don't think I could come back and do this again. Finish it now."

"One sec," I tell her, going to the sink and grabbing a washcloth down from the cabinet, wetting it under the cold water.

I place it on her forehead, to which she sighs and then smiles. "That feels so good. Thank you. So much better."

"I'm going to do this as fast as possible." It's getting tough for me to watch her in so much pain. But she's sat through every second without whining, which is impressive because I've seen some burly-ass men turn into the biggest pansies under my needle.

"Pain is a state of mind, Mello. I promise I'm fine. Just keep going," she reassures me.

And I do.

A FEW HOURS LATER, I'm wiping off her tattoo, and Arlo's skin is red and angry. Her body sags as soon as the word *Done* comes from my lips.

"How's it look?" she asks me, staring up at the ceiling, her skin covered in a slight sheen of perspiration.

"Stunning," I tell her, unable to take my eyes off my design gracing her body. "Want to see?"

"Yes," she whispers and starts to move.

"Go slow," I say, taking her hand to control how rapidly she gets up. I can't take my eyes off her as she makes her way to the mirror, staring at my mark on her skin.

"It's perfect. So perfect," she whispers, tears dotting her eyes. "I'm not sure I've ever seen something more beautiful."

"Me either," I murmur.

"Do you like it?" she asks, not hearing my comment.

"I love it, Arlo."

She turns, places her hands back on my bare shoulders, leans forward, and places her lips against my cheek.

I stop breathing, soaking in her softness and the sweet smell of her skin.

"Thank you," she murmurs against my ear.

My hands move to her hips, a completely inappropriate place for me to put them, but that doesn't stop me. "You're welcome, but thanks aren't required. I just want you happy."

"I am happy, and I'm excited for what comes next."

"What comes next?" I ask, going stupid.

"Our date."

I nod, dropping my hands. "Right." I clear my throat, hoping to God she doesn't see the wood I'm sporting and trying like hell to cover. "When?"

"I'll call you."

"Okay." I smile, moving my stool away from her and out of her intoxicating orbit. "Let me wrap you up and get you out of here."

"Sure," she says, lifting her arms, giving me the most spectacular view of her stomach, tits, ribs…all places I want to explore with my tongue.

I've never wrapped someone up so quick, going over the directions, and sending them out the door. Instead of taking her to the front desk myself, I call Lily to the room to do it for me.

Lily pops her head inside, her eyes widening when she sees me shirtless. "What the…"

"It's not what you think," I reassure her, lifting my hands.

She flattens her lips. "Really?"

Arlo laughs as she grabs her book from the table. "Lil, he was a complete gentleman. I asked him to keep his shirt off so it would be fair."

Lily's eyes move to Arlo and brighten. "If you say so," Lily says, but I know she's judging me. "Come on. I'll check you out."

"It's on the house, Lil. Don't charge her."

"I'm paying. I insist. You already paid for my car. I can't let you pay for the tattoo."

"Nope." I shake my head. "My treat."

Arlo smiles and thankfully doesn't argue with me. "I'll pay you back," she promises.

"I'm sure we'll find another way for you to compensate me."

Preferably by letting me explore her body, but since she's allegedly a virgin, that would be highly unlikely. But that doesn't mean I won't try.

Lily glares at me, her lips twisting, but Arlo's all smiles. "See you soon, Mello," Arlo says before giving me another quick kiss on the cheek and leaving the room with my cousin.

I sit there, staring at the door, and I know this is all going to go very, very wrong.

9

FORTY-EIGHT HOURS HAVE PASSED SINCE ARLO WALKED out of Inked, promising to call, but my phone hasn't rung.

The worst part is, I've been waiting.

I have never been the one to sit around, staring at my screen, trying to will the other person to call.

Is this how all the chicks in my life felt before?

God, I was such a dick.

It's a shitty feeling, filled with self-doubt, self-deprecation, and self-loathing. I've hit every stage, though briefly, over the last two days.

When I can't wait any longer, I grab my phone, quickly sending a message to Lily to see if the game has changed.

Me: Hey.

I immediately regret the message. The bitterness

coating the back of my throat only grows as I stare at the empty screen, waiting for a reply.

"I'm a moron," I whisper, tossing my phone on the bed to get ready for a night out.

There is no way I'm going to sit around on a Friday night, jerking myself off, waiting for a woman to call. I gave Lily my word, but so far, Arlo is the one in breach of contract.

But when my phone dings, I dive-bomb onto the bed, scooping up the sucker as quickly as possible.

Lily: Hey.

Me: How are you?

I have to make some small talk. Jumping right into asking about Arlo will be tipping my hand, and I never like to do that, even if it involves family.

Lily: Um, good. U?

Me: Great. Great.

Lily: What's up?

Me: Why does anything have to be up?

Lily: You rarely text me outside the group chat.

Me: I'm turning over a new leaf.

Lily: You're waiting for Arlo, aren't you?

Me: No.

Lily: Liar.

That text is followed by a winky face on Lily's end and a slew of curse words on mine. I hate that she knows me so well. She shouldn't. She's the sweetest and most innocent one in the family, but she and I click for some strange reason. I think it's her insatiable need to fix things, including people.

Me: Heard from her?

Lily: Have you?

Me: Fuck. Would I be asking you if I had?

Lily: Interesting.

Me: What's interesting?

Lily: Arlo not texting you.

I roll onto my back, throwing more than a few "motherfuckers" out there because my cousin is trying my patience, and I can guarantee she's laughing her ass off, too.

Me: Never mind.

Lily: Mello.

Me: This was the dumbest idea ever. I don't know how you talked me into it.

Lily: Cause you're old and need to settle down.

I blink, snarling at the screen as she uses my own words against me.

Me: I'm not old, and I do NOT need to settle down.

Lily: You said that, though. You said you were "old and tired."

Me: I needed a nap, babe. Not a new life.

I'm fucking lying, and she's calling me out. Lily forgets nothing. Never has and never will. The girl's mind is like a steel trap, mining little gems when she needs to remind us of our bullshit.

Lily: You want a family someday, right?

My mind goes there, and I let it. But the most fucked-up part is it's Arlo holding a green-eyed little girl, the spitting image of her mother, lying next to me. I shake my head, ridding myself of that insane thought.

Me: Someday. I still have a solid decade left in me, though.

Lily: A decade? You'll be 40.

Me: And...

Lily: You want more than one kid?

Me: Fuck if I know. I'll have whatever she wants.

Lily: Then you better get on that, Casanova, cause you're not getting any younger. And your shit may work now, but eventually, it'll give out like an old engine.

I read her message more than once with my fingers hovering over the buttons, formulating my reply.

Me: Men don't have an expiration date, Lil.

Lily: Oh. Guess what?

Me: What?

Lily: Arlo's calling. Hang on.

Me: What's she saying?

Lily: Hello.

Me: No shit. What else?

Lily: Shut up so I can talk to her. Jesus.

Me: Mention me.

I groan and drop my phone next to me, wanting to punch myself in the face. I'm a needy twat. Two days after being exposed to the woman again, and I've turned into a different person.

Lily: She's going to text you.

Me: When?

Lily: Settle down, rover.

Me: Fuck it. I'm going out.

Lily: Don't you dare.

I head for the bathroom, ready for a shower, when my phone dings. I ignore it, turning on the water instead. Then, there's not just one ding but an entire series of them, sounding like the worst song beat ever.

I give in, swiping across the screen, and the messages start scrolling by in rapid-fire succession.

Lily: He said he's going out because he's had to wait two entire days for Arlo.

Gigi: Don't you fucking dare ruin this.

Tamara: Pansy.

Gigi: Boys are weak.

Tamara: He's so, so, so weak.

Lily: It's kind of sweet.

Me: I'm here, assholes. I can see what you say.

Gigi: And?

Tamara: So. We'd say it to your face too.

Mammoth: You ladies are fucked up. Leave the guy alone. He was perfectly happy before y'all stuck your noses in his business.

Tamara: Honey...shut up. He was not. Were you happier before me? Let's be real about that. No one gave it to you as good as I do, baby.

Mammoth: ...

Pike: Oh fuck.

Gigi: That's some loud silence.

Tamara: That's because he's currently stalking my way, undoing his belt.

Gigi: Hot.

Lily: Why?

Tamara: Girl, read spicier books.

Lily: Duh. I do read spicy books.

Pike: Everyone leave Mello alone. He likes his life. Women always want to change a man. It's like a life's quest.

Lily: I'm talking to Arlo.

Tamara: And?

Gigi: Don't you have an ass to get spanked, Tam?

Tamara: I'm multifaceted.

Gigi: You can suck dick and text? I'm seriously impressed.

My cousins make my head hurt.

Rocco: I'm horrified.

Pike: Why?

Rocco: The girls are worse than us, bro.

Pike: Was there any doubt?

Rocco: Brother, when are you hooking up with Arlo?

Lily: She hasn't even called or texted him yet.

Pike: Not a good sign.

Gigi: She's playing him right.

I shake my head, hating all of them.

Me: No one's playing me, especially not Arlo. She's not that type.

Mammoth: Bro, you sitting there with your dick in your hand tonight?

Gigi: Ew.

Tamara: Mammoth.

Mammoth: What, babe? Serious question. Either he's out, searching for tail, or he's home, waiting for Arlo with his dick in his hand. He's a man. He's not sitting on the couch watching some sappy chick flick, crying tears.

Pike: Carmello never waits around for pussy.

Pike is technically right. At least, the old me never would have. But this me, the one who's laid eyes on and touched Arlo, is very much sitting around with his dick in his hand…and I hate him.

Gigi: We're more than pussy.

Pike: You ain't got a dick.

Gigi: How are you my husband?

Pike: Because I got that dick you like, darlin'.

Me: There comes a point where we cross a line as a family and hit TMI. We hit it.

Lily: Oh.

Me: Oh?

Gigi: Oh?

Tamara: Oh?

Nick: You all need a life.

Pike: For fuck's sake.

Me: Is this what married life is like, 'cause you're all super lame.

Tamara: Yeah, but we all got fucked tonight. Did you?

Me: Again, TMI, asshat.

Mammoth: Who'd you fuck?

Tamara: Shut up, baby. Stop playing games.

Mammoth: Wait until the kids go to sleep. You're getting it again.

Tamara: You making me a promise?

Me: STOP.

Gigi: Mello's grouchy.

Nick: Blue balls are setting in.

Rocco: I don't think he's gone this long without getting laid in his entire life.

Me: Lies.

Rocco: In the last eleven years, what was your longest dry spell?

I know the answer to his question. It was after Carrie died. She and I were never exclusive, but losing her tore me up. I had a very brief period when I didn't sleep with anyone because I felt dirty, like I was sullying her memory, and my head was so fucked up, I couldn't even look at a woman without thinking of her.

Me: You guys can all fuck off.

Gigi: Imagine what he's going to be like after a month.

Pike: He'll never last that long.

Rocco: I'll throw a hundred on that.

Mammoth: Me too.

Gigi: Seriously?

Nick: He can't last a week.

Rocco: I know my brother as well as I know myself, and the only thing he loves more than pussy is a challenge.

Jo: What the actual fuck? I walk away from my phone for five minutes... I'll put two hundred on that.

Nick: Bad bet, babe.

Rebel: Horrible bet. He was about to head out the door, and it's been forty-eight hours.

Me: I was not.

I turn off the water and step away from the shower, cursing at them under my breath.

Lily: I'm off the phone now.

Gigi: I can't believe how well you can text and talk.

Tamara: She's like superwoman.

Me: What'd she say?

Rebel: He's a goner.

Pike: Totally.

Mammoth: Done.

Me: Jesus-fucking-Christ.

Gigi: Better lock that shit down.

Me: We're not in a relationship.

Gigi: I know. That's why I said lock it down.

Me: It's fake, cousin. It's all part of Lily's fact-finding, fix-Mello mission.

Tamara: Uh-huh.

Gigi: Feels kinda real. I can hear you panting from here.

Me: <insert middle finger>

Lily: I'm calling you.

Gigi: Me?

Tamara: Me?

Rebel: Me?

Jo: Me?

Me: I hate you all.

Rocco: Nah, man. You love us, but right now, you're loving on Arlo the most.

Me: I don't think it was right for Lily to put her in the middle of all this. I don't really even know her.

Rocco: But ya want her.

I roll my eyes and my phone goes black, then Lily's name flashes across the screen.

"Ignore them," she says as soon as I answer. "They're stupid."

"What'd she say?"

"No hello. No how are you. Not even, you're the best cousin, Lily. Just, what'd she say?"

"Lily," I warn, my patience wearing thin.

Lily giggles. "Someone's not chill about this. I see she left an impression on you."

"I saw her tits. Of course she did."

"What the hell were you two doing in there with both of your shirts off?"

"She wanted to see my dragon."

"Carmello."

"The one on my back, goofball. I showed her, and she asked me to keep my shirt off. I can't help that she wants to stare at something beautiful. Now, what did she say?"

Lily's chuckle doesn't escape me. She's loving this and does nothing to hide her sheer enjoyment of my misery. "She only had good things to say, cousin."

"You're not giving me much, babe."

"I know." I can practically hear her smile on the other end of the phone. "She didn't say much. She said she was going to call you and that time got away from her. She wanted to make sure you were still a go."

My stomach flutters, and I'm instantly turned into a pubescent teenage girl. "I'm a go. Totally a go."

"I'm glad she called. I was worried that you'd somehow offended her. Figured if you were a complete douche, she wouldn't want to move forward."

"But she wants to, yeah? I may only think with my dick sometimes, but I'm never a douche."

"I bet there're some women out there who would disagree," Lily tells me. "Anyway, she's going to call. She just wanted some more info on caring for her tattoo. Her skin is tender."

"As it would be," I reply, knowing the soreness after having more than a few hours under the gun on my own ribs.

"She's just been lying low, letting herself heal. But tonight, she's feeling better and wanted to touch base with you."

"Lily," I whisper and swallow.

"Yeah, Mello?"

"I don't like where this is going," I admit, collapsing back onto my bed.

"Why?" she asks, sounding all innocent.

"You're both playing me, and I never get played. You couldn't find someone I'd never met to do this with me? Why her?"

"Why not her?"

"Because she's pretty and we know each other."

"Sometimes you have to beat a man at his own game for him to see a little more clearly."

"My eyes are fuckin' wide open, babe. Wide fucking open. You're not playing fair, and neither is Arlo."

"You catchin' feelings?"

"No," I snap.

"You are."

"I spent a little over five hours with the chick. I don't catch feelings in five hours."

"Meh," she mutters. "Feelings happen, and there's no reasoning why or how long until they do."

"There're no feelings, cousin. I caught attraction."

"Whatever. This is good."

"Good?" I ask, pulling the phone away to stare at it. "What do you mean, good?"

"Arlo isn't looking for a relationship."

"Wait." I sit up. "You set me up in a fake relationship, to figure out why I can't be in a relationship, with a chick who isn't looking for a relationship?"

"Yeah."

"Yeah?"

"Yeah."

"What the fuck, Lil? Do you hear how fucked up that is?"

"It's safer for you both."

"Safer?"

"Neither of you is ready for feelings or relationships, but I needed intel and Arlo is the best one to get that. She's putting herself out there, even in a fake way, because she feels safe to do so."

"Safe?"

"Not my story to tell, honey."

"What?"

"I've got to run. It's getting late. Arlo will text you soon."

"Like tomorrow or tonight?"

"Don't know. She only said soon."

"Fucking hell."

"Sucks having to wait for something you want, doesn't it?"

"You're an asshole," I tell her.

"I learned from the best, li'l cousin. Love you."

"Love you too," I grumble before the line goes dead.

Pike: Tomorrow night beers at the Cowboy. We need a night out.

Mammoth: I'm game.

Tamara: In.

Gigi: So ready.

Nick: We're in too.

Jett: Us too.

Rocco: We could use a night away from the kids. Mello, you in?

Me: I'll fucking be there.

Mammoth: Grouchy bastard.

Me: Fuck off.

Mammoth: I take it the bitch didn't call?

Tamara: Say that again. I dare you.

Mammoth: I stand corrected. I take it the lady hasn't called?

Tamara: Better.

Mammoth: Forgot we were among ladies.

Gigi: Where's ladies? I remember hearing Tam slobbered on your knob pretty fucking quick. That doesn't make a lady but a…

Tamara: Asshole, you literally left a bar with a man you didn't know, let him sink into you for almost a week, ghosting us, and then ended up with his ring on your finger. You do not get to judge.

Me: Y'all are giving me a headache. I'm out.

Jo: Go get her, big man.

Nick: <raised eyebrow>

Jo: What? He's big.

Nick: Jo baby, you better brace yourself because I'm about to show you a monster.

Gigi: <eye roll>

I hit close on the text thread, letting them go back and forth with their bullshit without me being a party to their insanity.

I swing my legs over the bed, ready to get up and get the fuck out, when my phone rings.

"Hello."

"Mello." Arlo's voice washes over me, knocking me backward.

"Hey, Arlo."

"Sorry I didn't call earlier."

"No worries," I lie. "I wasn't expecting you to call so soon anyway."

"I haven't done much besides read, trying to keep my mind busy and off the pain."

"That bad?" I ask, genuinely curious and concerned. Two things I usually am not about a chick.

"Just tender and I can't get comfortable."

"Have you been cleaning it?"

"Yeah, I'm following all the directions."

I'm sure she is. I don't even know why I asked. If she's anything like my cousin, she's following each step carefully.

"You in the mood to go out?" I ask her, never shy and always upfront about what I want.

"No," she sighs. "I'm too sore for that, and it requires me getting dressed and putting on a bra."

My mind instantly fills with naked Arlo, wearing her glasses and nothing else, curled up in her bed, turning the pages. Nerdy-girl shit that, for some odd reason, suddenly drives me wild.

"Want company? I can pick up some takeout and bring it to you. Check your ink while I'm there, too."

God, I'm lame and I'm fishing, trying to make up reasons why she should say yes. I've never worked for a chick's time, and this one has me begging.

Get your shit together, man.

"I'd be down for that, but only if you bring Chinese and don't mind me looking like a total train wreck."

"I don't think that's even possible, Arlo."

"The Chinese or the mess?"

"The mess, babe. I'll make the Chinese happen. Text me what you want, and I'll be there within the hour."

"I'll do that, but be prepared for a messy bun and no makeup."

"Are you wearing your glasses?" I ask.

There's silence for a moment before she whispers, "Yes."

"What else are you wearing?"

"Carmello."

"Don't move," I tell her, hustling my ass off the bed. "I'll find out for myself. Scratch the hour, I'll be there in thirty."

"I'll be waiting," she says, and my dick gets hard.

As soon as the line goes dead, I glance down at my cock and know the night isn't going to go as he plans. "Down, boy," I tell him and then go about ignoring him.

Fucking Lily.

10

"I'm so full," Arlo says with her hand on her stomach, lying flat on her back while I sit on the floor next to her legs.

"I don't think I've seen a chick eat so much food, and I have some eaters in my family." I stare at her, still in shock at the way she polished off every bit of her food and then started on mine.

"I love to eat, but sometimes my body isn't friendly about it."

"Your body is great, babe."

"Thanks, Mello. That's sweet of you to say, but you don't need to flatter me."

"Not flattering, Arlo. Just telling the truth. You're absolutely beautiful. All of you. When was the last time you cleaned your ink?"

"A few hours," she whispers with a sigh. "I hate doing it because it sucks."

"Want me to do it for you? I have a pretty tender touch." I'm not doing this to be nice. I want to touch her, feel the softness of her skin, and be able to look at her body without having to worry about fucking up her tattoo.

She opens her eyes and tips her head down, staring at me. "You'd do that for me?"

I move onto my knees to look down at her. "I'm not being totally selfless, Arlo. I really want to touch you."

"I trust you," she whispers, her green eyes locked on mine. "You were nothing but a gentleman at work and the other times I met you."

"What's your endgame?" I blurt out.

She blinks. "My endgame?"

"Yeah, Ar. How did Lily rope you into this? I still can't figure out how she got me to agree to it, but now that I've spent more time with you, I'm totally game for whatever is going to happen next."

She pushes herself up, wincing as she does it. The sting is unmistakable, and I remember the soreness I felt for days afterward. She's tough, but that spot is just a different kind of misery.

I'm perched by her knees, staring up at one of the prettiest girls I've ever seen—and I've seen a fucking lot. She looks amazing in the black spaghetti strap tank and loose-fitting shorts I'd give my left nut to shimmy down her legs with my teeth.

"Do you believe in love?" she asks me, her face serious but sweet.

"I've watched people all around me fall in love. Everyone in my family has been married forever, and they're happy. I know it's possible. I just don't know if it's possible for me."

"I've spent my life reading romance books, where people meet their true love, change their colors, and live happily ever after. When Lily told me about you and how she thought you deserved that too, she told me she couldn't figure out why you were stuck."

I smile. "I'm not stuck. I made a life choice."

"To be alone?" she asks softly.

I shake my head. "I'm rarely alone."

She raises an eyebrow. "Meaningless sex doesn't count, Mello. Technically you aren't alone, but what about when you want to talk to someone because you're going through some shit and need a person to listen?"

"I have my family."

"Is that fair to them?"

"Fair?"

"They have their own things to deal with. Don't you ever get lonely at night when you're by yourself in bed?"

"I could have sleepovers, but I prefer not to have the ladies stick around."

She reaches out, brushing her fingers across my skin, scorching me with her featherlight touch. "I believe in true love. I believe there's someone out there for each of us. Lily wants that for you, and after meeting you, I want that for you too."

"But why?" I prod, inching my hand closer to her legs.

"Because we all deserve happiness." She smiles, her entire face lighting up.

"I'm happy."

She burrows her fingers into my hair, and I do everything in my power to not close my eyes and bask in her touch. "I know you are, but what if your happiness is only a small fraction of what you're missing?" she asks.

I stare at her, thinking about her words. "Can't miss what I don't know, babe."

"What would you be doing if you weren't sitting here with me right now?"

"I'd be at the bar, a club, or with some woman I plan on never seeing again."

She frowns. "That's sad."

"But I'm having a better time sitting here with you, talking and barely touching, than I would've had doing any of those things," I admit, without even thinking about what I'm saying. "You still haven't told me why you agreed to this yourself. It can't be only because you believe in happily ever afters and all that mumbo jumbo."

She drops her hands from my body, and I instantly miss her heat. "I've never been great at dating. I've always been too nervous about impressing the other person. I thought this would be great practice for me, too, without all the expectations."

"Babe."

"What?"

"You're not great at dating?" I raise an eyebrow.

"I'm awkward and have the worst taste in picking the right men."

"I haven't noticed you being awkward."

She smiles down at me. "I feel comfortable with you."

"You do?" I ask, furrowing my brows.

She laughs, moving her hand back to my hair, ruffling it between her fingers. "Yeah. We're just hanging out, pretending to be something so I can help you move toward your forever. I don't have to worry about you judging me for my lack of putting out. We have a history together, although short."

"Can I ask you about…"

"About my lack of sex?"

"Have you done anything with a man? Sorry. That's none of my business. You don't have to answer."

"No, it's okay." Her cheeks turn pink as she tucks a

lock of hair behind her ear. "Yes, Mello, I've done *things*."

"So, you've kissed someone?"

She nods. "A little bit more than that."

Her words make me proud and sad at the same time. Proud of her for sticking to her guns, which isn't easy in today's society. And sad because I know I am never going to experience her completely.

"In our fake relationship…"

"Yeah?"

"Can we kiss? I mean, maybe I can give you some pointers. We can help each other out instead of it being a one-way street."

She laughs softly. "You'd do that to help me out?"

I nod quickly. "I could be your coach in all things physical, and you can be mine in all the ways of love."

It doesn't hurt to ask, and I fully expect her to tell me to fuck off, but I hold my breath, praying she doesn't.

"Maybe… Can I think about it?"

"Sure. Totally. No pressure. I feel like I'm the only one taking, and I'm a giver."

She smirks, running her finger along the side of my face, sending chills down my spine. "I'm sure you are."

My dick twitches, and I know we're entering dangerous territory. "How about those ribs? We should get them cleaned so you're all set for the night."

I need to change the subject and stop thinking about

planting my lips on hers. It's been the only thing on my mind since she walked out of the shop two days ago, which is insane. I've never put this much thought into kissing a woman because it's kissing. Something I've done with at least a hundred different people or more. There'd been women I'd been with whom I didn't even kiss. I wouldn't allow it because I wasn't sure where their mouth had been last. The condom kept my dick safe, but there was nothing to keep my mouth protected from whoever's dick they'd had their mouth wrapped around recently.

"You don't have to do it," she tells me. "I can do it after you leave."

"I want to take a look and make sure it's healing well."

"If you want to. I don't want you to do anything you don't want to."

She's acting like it's a hardship to look at her body, which it's not. This is the closest I'm going to get to any type of action with Arlo tonight, and I am surprisingly okay and excited about it too.

"I just need to get some stuff to clean your skin."

"Grab a bowl in the kitchen, and soap and towels are in the bathroom, first door down the hall."

"On it," I tell her, brushing my hand against her knee as I rise from the floor. "Don't move."

I go into the kitchen first, grabbing a bowl she had

on a towel, drying on the countertop. When I turn around to head to the bathroom, I stop dead.

Arlo's lifting her tank top over her head. My breath hitches like I've never seen a half-naked woman before, or even Arlo, because I have. With the bra she wore to the shop, there hadn't been much that was covered.

My feet finally come unstuck, and I head toward the bathroom, moving faster than before.

Arlo's topless.

Topless.

Putting a few pumps of soap into the bowl, I add warm water and grab the soap dispenser and a washcloth and towel from the shelf next to the shower.

I catch a glimpse of myself in the mirror, wondering who the person is staring back at me. I've never hauled ass for a shot at seeing breasts. I don't even go to strip clubs with my friends because I can get the real thing in person without spending a ton of cash, and with an orgasm at the end.

By the time I make it back to the living room, Arlo's on her back, arm over her breasts, cupping one in her hand. "Is this okay?" she asks, looking up at me with such innocence.

"If you're comfortable, I'm okay with it," I tell her, sitting next to her hip on the couch.

"Nudity doesn't bother me," she says softly, staring at me with those green eyes that call to me.

"Clearly you're not shy."

"Modeling made it impossible for me to be shy or worried about someone seeing my body. When you have to get naked in a room filled with twenty people, you get used to being comfortable in your own skin really fast."

My stomach knots at the thought of all those people looking at her, seeing the beauty I see lying before me. "I wouldn't like that."

"Really? You seem really comfortable in your skin too."

"No, babe. I wouldn't like other men looking at your naked body—or women, for that matter."

Arlo smiles, blinking slowly. "That's kind of sweet, but that was my life when I was younger."

"I don't think I could deal."

"It's one of the reasons why I didn't date much. Men were only after me for my body, having seen the photos online, or they were in the industry. I wanted to find someone who loved me for me before I gave them all of me."

"Makes sense. Sit up, baby," I tell her, holding the towel. "I don't want to ruin your couch."

She does so without question as I fold the towel in half, placing it under her back near her ribs. This is going to be messy, and I plan on taking my time when doing it too.

"Be right back. I need to wash my hands, or else it's all for nothing."

She nods, her eyes following me as I walk back into the kitchen like my ass is on fire. I make quick work of washing my hands, careful to clean them thoroughly before I dare get near her ink.

I take a few deep breaths, have a short but important conversation with my dick about the importance of the fucker behaving while I'm so close to her. The last thing I need is a boner, especially when I have Arlo being sweet and opening up to me.

"Do not ruin this for me," I tell my dick as I scrub my hands together, cleaning between each finger. "I'll make you pay."

"What?" Arlo says from the couch.

"Nothing. Just talking to myself."

"Everything okay?"

"Great," I lie, drying my hands with some paper towels.

I walk back slower, concentrating on my breathing. Why in the hell did I do this to myself? She could've just as easily cleaned it herself. But no. My dumb ass had to offer my own hands, sliding them over her ribs near her breasts. Fucking moron.

Arlo hasn't moved. Her hand and arm still cover her breasts, with her stomach and ribs exposed. "Is this okay? Should I lie different?"

"No. You're perfect. Just relax and I'll be gentle."

"I know you will," she whispers, staring up at me with nothing but trust in those green eyes.

I dip my fingers in the water and hold my hand above her ribs, letting the drops fall onto her battered skin. She stirs when they land on her flesh, but she quickly stills. Her eyes never leave me, always watching as I grab the soap, pumping a few drops on my hands.

She bites down on her lip, unsure of what I'm going to do.

I touch her softly, barely letting the tips of my fingers graze over her flesh.

She sighs and closes her eyes. "That feels so good."

"I can do this as long as you want," I tell her, hating myself for it, too.

I'm fucking cock-teasing myself. What in the hell has gotten into me? I've never been this tender, sweet guy I am right now. It's like Arlo put some magic spell on me, making me into a man I've never been. Making me want to be a man I never thought I could be.

Get ahold of yourself, fool. You're a wild beast. A pussy connoisseur. Slayer of bitches. The man every man wants to be and the one every woman wants to be in her.

"Thank you for this," Arlo whispers.

My eyes follow my fingers as I trace the ink, making small circles, carefully coating her skin with soap. "It's no bother. It looks like it's healing great. A few more days and it won't even hurt anymore."

"Thank God," she says. "I haven't been able to sleep on my side since. I didn't think this out well enough."

"Can't you sleep on your other side?"

"My body just rolls that way. I can't stop myself."

"I completely understand. I'm a back sleeper, so the back tattoo was a son of a bitch. I was a miserable prick."

"I can only imagine how grumpy you were."

I gaze up, my eyes meeting hers. "It wasn't pretty."

She smiles and it meets her eyes, making my chest ache. "You're really good with your hands."

I raise my eyebrow. "Careful, Arlo. I only have so much control, and it's taking everything in me not to kiss you right now."

She pulls her lip between her teeth, holding the corner.

"Let me finish this, and no more talking."

She nods, not letting go of her lip, but she keeps those eyes on me.

I tear my gaze away, moving my eyes back to her skin, keeping my touch light.

After adding a little more soap and water, I slow my movements, deciding I'll enjoy the last time I'll probably be able to touch her skin. My fingertips glide over every inch, tracing the lines I created and marked her with forever.

"Carmello," Arlo whispers as I slow, knowing I'm stealing time.

"Yeah, babe?" I ask, not looking up.

"Want to watch a movie with me? Maybe we can cuddle up on the couch and put on anything you want."

Cuddle?

"I've had a shit day," she explains. "I could really use some company tonight."

I'd never been a cuddler.

I'd fucked chicks and very nicely and quickly escorted her or myself to the door, or wherever we were parting ways.

Cuddling has never been my style.

But right now, with Arlo's big, hopeful eyes staring at me and my fingers floating across her skin, I say, "Sure, sweetheart. Whatever will make you happy." She smiles, and my chest aches, in that same unfamiliar way it did earlier.

I am fucked.

11

My eyes pop open and my heart races, finding a woman wrapped around me, leg thrown over my middle, and arm slung across my chest.

For a second, I lie there perfectly still, too scared to move and confused about where I am.

Then it hits me.

Arlo.

The movie.

The cuddling.

The way she fit perfectly around my body, clinging to me during the scary bits and mindlessly running her fingers across my chest during the rest.

I liked it.

I liked it way too much.

We fell asleep like this, my eyes drifting closed before the movie ended. She's settled in on her side, tattoo side up, nuzzled between the back of the couch and my body.

It felt right and as if we'd done this forever. The very fake relationship has started to feel more real than anything I've ever experienced before, and in all honesty, it scares the ever-living shit out of me.

"Mello," Arlo whispers, her arm tightening across my upper body.

"Go back to sleep," I whisper back, squeezing her hip, the place my hand feels most at home.

"Want me to move?"

"No, babe, not unless you want to."

"I'm so comfy," she says in a sleepy voice, her arm going limp along with the rest of her. "So very comfy."

I turn my head, soaking in her pretty face, studying her features as she lies with her head on my shoulder, eyes closed. I stay like that, watching her until her breathing changes, each inhale growing longer as she slips into a deeper sleep.

An hour passes while I stare at her in the soft glow of the television, wondering what the fuck I'm doing here, snuggling with a woman I just met and have no hope of ever sinking into.

It's as if Arlo has cast some secret voodoo spell over me, and somehow, I allowed it to happen. I've been sucked in by the mysterious woman my cousin set me up with, and I've gone along for the ride, with my arms up, screaming into the wind at the top of my lungs, letting myself leap before I looked where I was going.

Leaning forward, I kiss Arlo's forehead, whispering a few words to her. I smell her skin, memorize the softness of her flesh against my lips, and slide out from under her.

I've already broken my rules. I stayed the night. I cuddled. We most certainly did not have sex. We didn't even kiss, but for some reason, guilt eats at my insides as I pull on my boots and slip out the front door.

"Fuck," I hiss into the early morning air, catching sight of the moon as it starts to set near the tree-filled horizon. Without looking back, I'm on my bike, heading toward home.

LILY'S WAITING for me at the front desk when I arrive at Inked. Her head comes up from studying the appointment book, but there's no smile on her face. "How did last night go?"

"Fine. Great." I smile, stalking into the front of the shop as the door closes behind me. "Nothing interesting to report."

Her blue eyes study me as she bites down on the pencil in her hands. "You sure about that?" she asks, the words garbled.

"Yep," I reply, keeping any type of tone out of my answer.

She reaches out, grabbing my forearm as I start to walk by her, and stops me from moving to the back. "And Arlo?"

I glance down to where our bodies are connected. "Still in one piece and just as I left her last night, I'd assume."

"You assume?" She raises an eyebrow. "And how did you leave her last night?"

"Ask Arlo," I tell her, yanking my arm free of her grip, and keep moving.

Lily's right behind me, her heels clicking away against the tile floor. The shop is still empty except for the two of us.

This is my week to open, but Lily has taken it upon herself to be here too, probably wanting to bust my balls and question me before the rest of the crew gets here. There is no probably about it—this is her only purpose for being here.

"I don't know why you're so grouchy. You asked me to do this. You asked for my help. You asked for me to set you up with a nerdy girl so you could broaden your horizons beyond your usual barflies."

I spin around, stopping in the middle of the workroom, and Lily practically runs into me. "I know I asked for your help, but Arlo and I have history, Lily," I groan, shaking my head. "She's almost perfect, and you did this shit on purpose to drive me fucking crazy."

Lily tips her head back, a smirk on her face. "Did you sleep with her last night?"

"Of course not. I'm not going to push her to do something that she doesn't want or isn't ready for."

"You kiss her?"

"No, Lily." I glance at the ceiling and sigh. "Not even a kiss."

Lily places her hands on my chest, looking at me like I'm sweet. "You're a good man, Mello. There's hope for you yet."

"What have you done to me?"

She giggles and pats my chest. "Nothing. You asked, and I delivered."

I narrow my eyes. "You're setting me up."

She lifts her hands in the air and takes a step back. "I'm doing no such thing. You asked for help, and I'm helping."

"You're ruining me," I grumble.

"Nah, cousin. I'm fixing you. We're rewiring your brain."

"My brain worked just fine before Arlo."

"Did it, though?" she asks, her voice filled with sarcasm.

I tilt my head, crossing my arms and continuing to stare at my cousin as she smiles.

"Hey," Gigi says, walking into the shop, and she

stops dead when she sees us. "Oh boy. What happened?"

"Mello is falling for Arlo," Lily tells her, not breaking eye contact with me.

"Am not," I argue.

"He so is," Lily returns. "Head over heels."

"Like fuck, I am." I growl those words.

Gigi's eyebrows rise as she throws down her purse and comes to stand by us. She looks at Lily and then to me, her lips tipping upward. "Did you fuck her yet?"

I roll my eyes. "Again, no."

"Kiss?" Gigi asks, going down the same route as the other one.

"No. Jesus, you two are a perfect match."

"How's he falling in love with her?" Gigi asks, looking back at Lily. "If he were, he'd at least touch her."

"Arlo said he stayed over last night and snuggled with her too."

Gigi's eyes grow wide. "You snuggled?"

I grunt. "I don't see what the big deal is."

Gigi mimics my stance, crossing her arms, head cocked to the side. "You don't snuggle. You don't do sleepovers either. You also fuck everything that walks."

"I checked on her ink, and we watched a movie and fell asleep."

"While cuddling," Lily adds.

I snarl. "Well, since we weren't fucking, I dozed off."

"Uh-huh," Gigi mutters, laughing and elbowing Lily. "He dozed off from boredom. Is that what he's saying?"

"Yep," Lily says with a small giggle.

I wave my hand at them and stalk toward my workstation. "You two can fuck off."

"He cleaned her tattoo and brought her Chinese, too," Lily tells Gigi.

"Did she tell you everything?" I ask, not bothering to look at them.

"No. I didn't know if you did anything more, but you confirmed it. She was cagey with her answer, which was odd."

"She was cagey?"

"Yeah." Lily shrugs. "Figured I'd get the rest out of her later since it's literally her job to get the goods on you."

"Right. I forgot," I mutter, honestly forgetting that nothing that was happening between us was real.

It felt real.

Every moment I had been with her felt natural and not like we were acting a part as practice for the big event with another person.

Being with Arlo is easy, and I hate her for it—and Lily too.

"Did you want to kiss her?" Gigi asks as she plops down in the chair nearest me.

"Fuck yeah. I'm not blind. She's gorgeous."

"She isn't your usual type," Gigi tells me. "But there were definitely some sparks when you brought her to Mammoth's shop to get her car."

"There were not, and I have no type, cousin."

She taps her chin, studying me. "If any woman is ready, willing, and able, along with having a very open vagina policy, you are game to hit that shit."

I cover my eyes with my hand, shaking my head, hating her and Lily right now. "Not with Arlo."

"And yet, you still went to her house," Gigi says. "You're smitten with her. Just admit it and save yourself some grief."

"It's fake, Gigi. I'm a pet project, and that's it, babe. Let's be real. A classy chick like Arlo isn't going to be interested in a guy like me."

"A guy like you?" she asks, jerking her head back, her eyebrows drawn down. "What the fuck does that mean?"

"She's like the best of the best, and I'm…"

"A playboy?" she asks.

"That's one way to describe me."

"You're a single guy who's living his life. There's no shame in that. Hell, Pike had a colorful past, and Jesus, look at Jett. We all have pasts, and they don't define the person we are or who we will be in the future."

"I don't know," I mutter.

"Do you truly like Arlo?" Lily asks me, coming to sit with us. "Like *like her, like her*?"

"I think so, babe. I don't know how I feel. Maybe my head's just foggy because I haven't fucked another chick and it's messing with my mind."

"Then go fuck someone else and see how you feel afterward," Gigi tells me like it's no big deal.

"Technically, it's against the agreement, but I've never seen you so grouchy and bent out of shape. Maybe you should. We can keep it our little secret," Lily says, touching my shoulder.

"I like that idea," Gigi agrees. "Go out tonight and see how you feel after. It may give you a new perspective on things."

"Wait. I have a better idea," Lily announces, her eyes widening before she claps her hands. "We'll meet you at the bar and bring Arlo. You do your thing, and we'll do ours. You'll figure out if she really has some pull over you, and we can see if she feels the same. She was a little weird on the phone earlier and had me wondering. So this will be perfect."

I stare up at her, confused as fuck. "You want me to hit on other women with Arlo watching? Do you even know how fucked up that is?"

Lily paces in front of me. "Just flirt with some girls,

be your usual self. I want her to see how you work a room."

"Dumbest shit I've ever heard," I grumble.

Gigi twirls around in her seat and comes to a dead stop, her boots slamming against the tile. "Have you ever seen one of the women you've slept with at a bar and still left with someone else?"

"Well, duh. There are only so many bars and women in this town."

She lifts her hands. "Point proven. Arlo shouldn't be any different from the others. You're not dating, and hell, you haven't even kissed her. It shouldn't be a big deal. Unless it is…"

"It's not," I bite out.

Gigi smiles. "We'll see."

"Absolutely not," I say, putting my foot down. "You're not bringing Arlo to watch me hit on random chicks, trying to get laid. That's not how shit is done, and it's not right. It's a hard no, and there's no debate. Got me?"

Gigi tilts her head, a small smirk twitching on her lips. "You hearin' this?" she asks Lily, but she keeps her eyes locked on mine.

"I am, and I'm shook."

Pike, Rocco, Rebel, and Trace walk into the shop, talking back and forth, shooting the shit, and come to a dead stop when they see the three of us.

"What'd we miss, because, by the looks of the standoff, it's a lot," Pike asks his wife.

"Tell them," I say, looking back and forth between Lily and Gigi. "Tell them all your amazing idea."

"We want Mello to go to a bar and do his normal thing."

"Which is?" I ask, because she's being evasive with her answer for a reason.

"A one-night stand," Gigi replies.

"And this is a problem because…?" Rocco asks me, but I point to Lily.

Lily sighs. "Because we want to bring Arlo to watch."

The three guys all jerk their heads back, understanding the problem without knowing the full extent of the fucked-upness of it all.

Lily's officially lost her mind. In what alternate reality is her idea a good one? None. Fake dating or not, I don't want Arlo to watch me hitting on and trying to tag other women. That shit isn't cool, no matter the circumstances.

"Bad idea," Rocco mutters, rubbing the back of his neck. "Really bad."

"Super fucked up, babe. You don't do that shit," Pike adds, confirming my feeling.

"Sounds like a delicious recipe for a catfight. I'm there for whatever happens," Trace announces. "Count me in."

Rebel rubs her temples before covering her face with her hands. "You two come up with the craziest shit," she mumbles, talking to Gigi and Lily but not looking at them when she says those words.

"It's a fact-finding mission, and this is why Arlo's here. I don't get the big deal," Gigi tells everyone. "Let's remember, they're not dating. It's all fake to teach Carmello how to land a forever relationship."

"Still fucked up," Pike tells her. "You don't have the new piece of ass, real or not, watch you find a different piece of ass, without causing a whole lot of headache and misery."

"Fake ass shouldn't have an opinion on or be an issue for the real ass," Gigi replies.

I shake my head, questioning my life choice to work with my nosy-ass family and for getting Lily involved in my personal life.

"Wait," Rebel says, and I close my eyes. "I'm getting a vibe."

"There's no vibe," I tell her, lifting up my hands and leaning back into my chair. "None. Zero. Zilch."

She smiles. "You like this woman. Like really, really, really like her."

"I don't."

"It wasn't a question," she says. "You do. Because you've never cared about feelings or blowback when it came to any other piece of ass."

"Can we stop saying piece of ass?" Lily asks, having

all sets of eyes turn to her. "I mean, she's our friend, and we know she's more than that."

"I'm with Lily. Be respectful."

"Right now, she's tail," Pike argues. "Unless there's something you aren't telling us."

"There's nothing," I say, pushing my chair back and getting up. "Drop it."

Everyone's quiet, staring at me with their mouths open.

"Oh boy," Pike mumbles.

"Yep," Rocco adds.

"Shit, he's gone," Rebel says. "Knew it."

"Totally," Gigi says with a smile. "I told you this would happen."

"Fuck that," Trace tells them then turns his gaze on me. "You need a wingman tonight, I'm there."

I turn, glaring at them all. "Everyone can fuck off."

Gigi places her hand on her chest, leaning back. "Touchy bitch, ain't he?"

Lily pulls out her phone. "Let's get another opinion."

"What are you doing?" I ask her, everyone's eyes on her as she lifts the phone to her ear.

Lily waves me off. "Hey, Arlo."

"No," I whisper, moving toward her, but she spins, holding the phone away as I try to snatch it.

"You want to go out tonight and grab a drink?" Lily smiles, staring at me as she listens to Arlo's answer.

"It'll be later, after I finish my last appointment. I'll bring my cousins too."

"Fuck," I mutter, glancing upward.

"I'm in for a ladies' night," Rebel says.

"Who said it was ladies only?" Rocco asks. "I thought we agreed it would be all of us."

"I just want a night out. I don't care who's there," Gigi tells everyone.

"No. He won't be there." Lily smiles, waggling her eyebrows at me. "He has *other* plans."

I roll my eyes.

"You still game?" she asks Arlo and pauses, the room quiet, waiting for the reply. "Perfect. I'll text you where and when later today."

"I'm not telling you where I'm going," I tell Gigi immediately, letting her know their scheme isn't going to go as planned.

"Whatever," she says, looking smug. "I want to see Arlo, not spend time with you."

The sad thing is, I want to see Arlo too, and I hate myself for it.

12

Gigi: You bitches coming?

Lily: Almost there.

Tamara: Parking.

Jo: Nick's driving like a snail.

Gigi: You got Arlo?

Lily: No. She said she didn't feel well.

I stop moving, having found out what I needed to know.

Arlo didn't go with them and is at home…alone.

A second later, I open a new text, shooting off one to her.

Me: Hey, Ar. How're your ribs?

Arlo: Better.

I wait for more, but nothing comes.

Me: You pissed at me?

Arlo: No.

Another one-word answer. She's pissed. I've been around enough women in my life to know the difference.

Me: Sorry I left before you woke up. Had to get home and ready for work.

Arlo: No big deal. You don't owe me an explanation.

Me: Want me to come over?

Arlo: Not tonight.

So, "no big deal" is a lie. It is a big deal to her, and although she says I don't owe her an explanation, the one I gave her isn't good enough.

Me: Tomorrow?

Arlo: I'll let you know.

Yep. Pissed.

Me: Got it. Sleep well. Talk soon, babe.

Arlo: Night.

I immediately close that text and open back up the group text with my cousins, having missed dozens of texts in the last few minutes.

Me: Where are you assholes?

Gigi: Neon Cowboy.

I roll my eyes. Not my typical haunt, but it is good in a pinch. The women are…different from my normal taste.

But pussy is pussy, and they serve a cold beer.

Me: On my way.

Mammoth: Someone got cockblocked.

Pike: Totally shutdown.

Me: Can't shut down what isn't real, jagoffs.

Gigi: Oh boy. Someone's butthurt.

I grab my keys, pull on my boots, ignoring their bullshit. They're going to talk shit about me until I get there, so there's no use in replying.

The roads are empty as I make my way to the little bar in the middle of nowhere. The entire ride, I only think about Arlo and how I have fucked up. But I'm not going to let myself feel guilty about leaving her place without saying goodbye. We are nothing to each other, not even friends. We are an arrangement with no promises.

"Fuckin' A," Mammoth says as I make my way through the crowded bar, heading straight to the back where they always sit. "'Bout time, brother."

"I wasn't planning on coming," I tell him, grabbing a chair and spinning it around before straddling the back.

"You were, but not here," Rocco adds, giving me a chin lift, laughing his ass off at my expense.

"Fuck off," I tell him.

"You need this more than me," he says, pushing a fresh beer in front of me.

"I thought for sure you'd be with Arlo tonight and not here since you made such a stink at work earlier," Gigi tells me, snuggling up to Pike's side.

"She's sick, babe. Lily put that in the text."

"That's what she said, but is she really?" Gigi stares

at me, her lips flat. "You go to her place one night, and the next, she's *sick*."

"Happens," I mutter, lifting the bottle to my lips.

"What did you do to her?" Lily asks me.

I shrug, beer to my lips. "Why did I have to do something?"

Lily leans forward, elbows on the table and hands clasped. "You stayed overnight at her place, and tonight she's still weird. Are you sure you didn't take things too far?"

"Can't believe you're asking me that shit, babe," I mumble against the rim.

She crosses her arms and stares right back. "When was the last time you slept at a woman's house?"

"Never."

She cocks her head to the side and raises an eyebrow. "But you slept at Arlo's?"

I guzzle half the beer before wiping my lips with the back of my hand and grunt, "Yep."

"Wait." Mammoth shifts, moving Tamara back in his embrace and turning to face me fully. "So, you slept at the chick's house and didn't bang her?"

"We've been over this," I tell him before downing the rest of my beer.

"Some of us don't work at Inked, bro. I hear everything hours later and secondhand."

"Didn't kiss her either," Gigi adds, making a face when she says that too.

Mammoth slides his eyes from me to her. “No shit?”

“No shit,” she replies.

He slides his eyes back to me. “No action at all and you slept over. What the fuck, man? Your shit broke?”

“Nope,” I growl.

“Head’s fucked up, though,” Nick tells him. “She’s got him all twisted.”

“Sounds like you not too long ago,” Mammoth says to Nick, smiling. “Told ya, and you didn’t see the light until you were sunburned.”

“Have you hit your head recently?” I stare at Mammoth, blinking a few times.

Mammoth’s jaw ticks as he moves a toothpick around his mouth. “No. You?”

Nick runs his hand down his face, peering at Mammoth over his palm. “No, but you keep talking like you’ve been reading riddles all of a sudden, and it’s weird as fuck, man.”

Mammoth laughs. “Sounds better than saying I told you so, but I told you so.”

Nick nods. “True that.”

“But you,” Mammoth says, pointing at me with a beer in his hand. “You’re fucked, brother.”

I jerk my head back, furrowing my brows. “How am I fucked?”

“A chick already got you acting like another person.”

“No,” I snap.

"Yeah, he is," Gigi says, laughing.

He keeps that finger pointed at me when he says, "Just lock that shit down and move the fuck on with life."

"Lock it down?" I ask.

Pike nods. "Yep. It's easier if you come to terms with it now. Accept your fate and then move forward."

"I've literally known the woman a few days," I argue. "I'm not locking shit down. It's not even a real relationship or friendship. I'm a test subject."

"Whatever," Pike mutters. "I saw the way you two looked at each other."

"Means nothing," is my only answer.

"I still can't figure out how Arlo went from piping-hot to ice-cold in a flash, Mello. What really happened?" Lily presses me.

"Lily, swear to God, I didn't do shit. We fell asleep, and then I hustled my ass out of there before she woke up."

Lily makes a face, sucking in air between her teeth. "You just left?"

I nod. "What the fuck else was I supposed to do?"

"Idiot," Lily whispers.

"Total dumb-ass move," Gigi adds.

"Fucking moronic," Tamara says.

Rebel nods. "Fucked up big, brother."

"Men are so clueless." Jo throws in with the other insults being hurled my way.

I glare at them as they sit in judgment, but their men remain silent. "What was I supposed to do? Wake her up and tell her thanks for the movie?"

"Did you at least leave a note?" Jett asks, suddenly finding feelings and adding something to the conversation.

"Uh, no." I roll my eyes, polishing off the last sip of beer before motioning to the waitress and pointing at the table.

"Yeah, you fucked up," Jett whispers, reaching behind his wife to stretch his arm across her chair. "You can't just sneak out and then ghost a chick."

"I didn't ghost her. I texted her before I came here."

"Did you text her at all earlier in the day?"

"No," I bite out. "We've been over this shit a million times."

"Yep, fucked up big," Jett mutters.

I'm done with their bullshit. I refuse to allow them to make me feel guilty about something I did that wasn't wrong. There was no way I was going to wake up a sleeping Arlo before I left. If she were my girl, maybe, but it isn't my style. And since the deal was not to treat her any differently than I would any other woman, I left without saying a word.

"I'm having the next one at the bar," I announce, pushing my chair back and standing. "You can all fuck off and talk about me, but I'm going over there—" I tick my head back "—and finding a piece of ass to bury myself in tonight."

"Classy," Lily whispers, peering up at me with her judgy blue eyes. "But you should—"

"Save it," I cut her off, waving my hand. "Whatever you're going to say, I don't want to hear it."

She purses her lips and narrows her eyes. "But—"

"No, Lily. You've done enough."

Jett stiffens.

"No disrespect, cousin, but I need to blow off some steam and get my head right. I love you, Lily, but butt the fuck out." As soon as the words are out of my mouth, I'm making my way toward the bar, winding through the people.

The waitress sees me, depositing the beer in front of me before the bartender has time to make it to me.

"Thanks, doll." I smile at the older woman.

She smiles back. "Welcome, sweetie."

I watch the flat screen, unable to hear the muted conversation of the sports announcers but giving no shits because at least they aren't chirping in my ear about all the ways I've fucked up like my own family.

A person walks up to the bar and slides onto the barstool next to where I stand, brushing their elbow against me.

I turn my head, going in for a quick glance as I retract my elbow, and I am caught by surprise. The woman is mint in that rough, badass biker girl kind of way. Harley tank, tons of cleavage, teased hair, and lots of makeup, looking like she is out to give exactly what I want to take.

I smile at her, giving her my classic chin lift. "Hey."

She glances my way, her lips tipping upward before she moves her eyes down my face to my arms, taking her sweet-ass time. "Hey yourself, handsome."

"Can I buy you a drink, beautiful?"

She nods, her big brown eyes locked on my biceps as I move. "Tequila on the rocks," she whispers, barely loud enough for me to hear over all the noise around us.

"Tequila it is," I tell her, motioning for the bartender and giving him her order.

"Aside from being sexy, what do you do for a living, honey?" she asks me, totally thirsty for my body, which I am perfectly fine with.

I laugh, liking how she's forthright. I know she wants me and that I could fuck her right now if I wanted to. That I have no doubt about. If I invited her to the bathroom, pinned her against the sink, she'd push her pussy against my cock, fucking herself if I let her. "Tattoos, babe."

Her eyes light up. "Sexy job for a sexy man," she says, taking the drink as soon as the bartender places it down in front of her. Within three seconds, the glass is to her lips and the liquid is gone.

"So, tell me, what's a handsome thing like you doing in a place like this?"

"Could ask you the same thing, sweetheart. A girl as pretty as you should have herself a man to be at home with, sucking and fucking all night."

Jesus.

I almost roll my eyes at myself, but she smirks, looking at me like a meal.

"Trying to get over a broken heart," she tells me, and I know I've got her.

Nothing says easy pussy like rebound pussy. This chick wants to be filled, having all the memories of her last dick wiped out by a new one.

"You lookin' for help, sugar?"

"I put out my help wanted sign." She waves her hand over her very large and visible breasts. "Think you're up for the job?"

My eyes move to her breasts, studying them, knowing they'd be heavy in my palms. But I'm not here to worship her body. I am here to forget someone else's. I lean forward, my face in her wild hair, and whisper against her ear, "I could fill the position."

She shivers, moving her mouth to my ear. "I may have an opening," she whispers before her tongue comes out and strokes my earlobe.

And then Arlo's face and pretty smile flash through my head.

Fuck.

"I can't," I tell her, pulling away. "I can't do this."

Goddamn it.

This woman is a sure fucking thing, and I can't do it. Arlo and I are nothing to each other, but somehow she's between me and a night of pussy. Easy pussy, but still pussy.

"Your dick broke?" she asks, tilting her head and narrowing her eyes.

"No," I growl and grab my beer. "Dick's working fine. It's my head that's fucking me up."

"Don't need to think to fuck, babe."

I shake my head. "When my head's thinking about another chick, it's not a good policy to fuck a different one. Sorry to waste your time."

She gives me a sorrowful smile. "It's okay."

"You have a good night," I tell her, tipping my chin to her before stalking back toward the table.

"What the fuck just happened?" Pike asks before my ass has a chance to make contact with the seat bottom.

"Fuck," I groan, running my hand down my face. "I don't know."

"Arlo," Lily teases, smiling like an idiot because she did this to me.

She broke my dick by setting me up with Arlo, tempting me with her sweetness when I've become used to so much bad.

"You're right," Mammoth adds, lifting his beer to his lips. "You are *fucked,* and that shit happened quick. Welcome to the party."

"Baby." Tamara turns to her husband, placing her

hand over his as it rests on the table. "The party can end pretty fucking quick if you're not satisfied with the guest list."

Mammoth smirks, locking his fingers with hers. "Princess, shut it."

Tamara's head jerks back. "Excuse me?"

"There isn't anyone else in the world I'd put up with on a daily basis except you. I'm right where I want to be, and I happily accepted that fate years ago. But your cousin over there acts like he has some choice in the matter, when his head and heart are already playing tricks on him."

"That was kind of sweet."

"I have everything I want in the world—a wife, kids, a business—but Carmello is just now coming to terms with the simple fact that life needs to be filled with more than easy pussy."

"In the name of honesty, Tamara was easy pussy," Gigi adds with a snort.

Tamara's eyes snap to Gigi and narrow. "Um, you literally had your mouth wrapped around a stranger's dick within an hour of meeting him."

Pike smiles. "That stranger was happy too."

"Stop," I mutter, not wanting to hear their mushy bullshit. "I'm not in love with Arlo."

"Didn't say love, brother," Mammoth says. "But she's under your skin, and there's no easy way of getting her out. It's best to just give in and see where the shit lands in the end."

"Fuckin' great," I grumble against the rim of my beer, glaring at Lily. "You did this."

She lifts her hands, giving me an innocent smile. "I did nothing. I put someone in your path, but the rest is all you, cousin."

"I've been in your shoes, man," Jett tells me with his arm slung around Lily's chair. "Just give in and let whatever's about to happen, happen, or you're going to be one miserable bastard."

"I already am," I mumble against my beer, knowing Arlo's already fucked with my head.

13

AN HOUR LATER, I'M STANDING ON THE FRONT STEP OF Arlo's place, hands tucked in my pockets, waiting for her to answer.

The front light is turned on, and then nothing for a few seconds before she says, "What are you doing here?" from the other side of the door.

I stare at the peephole, knowing she's looking at me. "Arlo, open up."

"I'm not decent."

I smirk. "And that's a problem, how?"

"It's late," she says, her voice muffled by the door, sounding a million miles away.

"We have shit that needs to be said."

"We do not," she shoots back immediately. "Go home, Carmello."

I rest my hands on either side of the door, moving

my face closer to try to see her inside, even though it's futile. "No, sugar. I'm not leaving."

"You had no problem leaving before."

Bing-fucking-o.

"Come on. Let me in to explain."

"Explain from there," she tells me.

I growl, gripping the frame tighter, and rest my head against the door. "I'll stand here until morning if I have to."

The light switches off, and I'm cast back into darkness. Un-fucking-believable. The woman has big-ass balls, and she is sporting them for me right now.

"Arlo," I beg, not hearing her walk away. "Please."

"Give me one good reason to let you in."

I let my head fall forward, holding on to the doorframe, my body stretched out and boots firmly planted on the cement. "I could've kissed a woman tonight. Hell, I could've fucked her in the bathroom."

"You're not winning me over," she interrupts.

I lift my head, staring straight into the peephole, and hope she can see my face. "The important word is *could've*."

"You should've," she bites out. "We're not in a relationship, Mello. You don't have any loyalty to me."

I take a deep breath, remembering Arlo doesn't know me and she's pissed. She's super pissed, in fact—not about the chick, but because I left without so much as saying goodbye. It was a dick move, especially since

I didn't contact her after either. "Fuck," I groan. "You know why I didn't, and you're pissed at me for the same reason."

"Nope," she clips. "And it's none of my business."

"I didn't and couldn't because, even with her in front of me, offering herself up on a platter, all I could see was your face."

"Am I supposed to be flattered by that?"

I peer up and grunt. "What are we, Arlo?"

"I don't know."

"What do you want to be?" I ask.

Silence.

"I thought we were going to be friends at the most—and at the very least, acquaintances—but fuck me, one night with you and…"

The door opens a few inches, and I see half her beautiful face, with her body hidden behind the door. "And?" she asks, her eyes staring into mine.

I don't let go or move a muscle but keep rolling with what I had been about to say before. "And you're the only thing I can think about. Do you know how fucked up that is for a guy like me?"

Even with only half of her mouth visible, I can see the small smile. "I'm sorry," she whispers. "Feel better now?"

"No," I snap. "We have to talk about us before we dig this ditch so deep, the depth becomes too high for us to crawl out."

She sweeps her gaze across my face. "What?"

"You're pissed at me for leaving last night."

"You mean this morning."

"Same thing, but you're pissed, right?"

She shrugs.

"You are, and I'm not leaving until we talk about why you're pissed and why I left."

"Carmello, it's been a long day, and I…."

"It's going to be a longer night if you make me keep standing out here."

She sighs before opening the door wide enough for me to come in.

"Thank you," I tell her, walking inside and immediately kicking off my boots.

When I turn around, she's standing with her head cocked, dark hair up in a messy bun, arms folded, and clearly still not happy with me.

"Stop being mad at me."

She purses her lips because my words don't resonate, and she isn't about to listen without explanation.

"Can I sit?"

"Yep. Sure. You're inside now. Might as well."

Her attitude level is maximum. I can't say I blame her with the way I ditched out, but that has always been my MO.

As soon as my ass touches the couch, I pat the cushion next to me. "Come closer."

She stares at me without so much as blinking.

"Please," I ask again.

She moves, and I can't keep my eyes off her legs in her tight yoga pants, revealing every inch of her body, along with a T-shirt cut just below her breasts, revealing her fresh ink.

"My eyes are up here near my ears," she says before collapsing onto the cushion next to me, quickly tucking one leg underneath, using it to keep a space between us. "You're here. Now, talk."

I mimic her position, turning to face her, leg tucked beneath me, but I sling my arm over the back of her couch. "You have my head twisted."

She cocks her head and furrows her brow. "How'd I do that?"

"I don't know." I shake my head slowly. "But you did. In the last twenty-four hours, I've done things I never thought I'd do."

"Like…" She dips her chin and waves her hand in between us.

"I've never slept at a woman's house."

Her shoulders drop, and I get the feeling she already thinks I'm lying. "Never?" she asks.

I shake my head. "I always left, or they did."

She makes a face. "How is that possible?"

"Baby, I wasn't there for a relationship. When we were done, it was over and time to go." I lift my hand from my leg. "I take that back. There was one girl I slept with, but that was over a decade ago. No one since."

Her mouth opens as she blinks at me, confused. "For real?"

"No lie."

"But we cuddled last night."

"Another thing you have me doing that I've never done before. I had never cuddled with anyone, especially someone I haven't fu…slept with."

"That's crazy. Cuddling is fantastic."

"Well, so are orgasms." I smile.

She doesn't return my smile. "There's more to life than sex."

I touch my chest, pretending to be shocked. "Obviously, you haven't had one that rocks you to your core."

"Well…" She clears her throat, shifting her body weight. "Obviously, you haven't had the right cuddle partner."

"I did last night," I tell her.

Her cheeks instantly turn pink, and she glances down. "But then you ran out of here like your ass was on fire and didn't bother to contact me all day. I figured I did something wrong."

I brush my fingers over her shoulder, and she doesn't move away from my touch. "That was about me, not you, Arlo. I was so comfortable with you, I fell asleep, and when I woke up…I freaked out and ran."

"Like a pussy," she mutters.

"What?"

"Nothing." She smiles, but it's a devilish look.

"It's like if you woke up naked after sleeping with a man you didn't know. You'd run, wouldn't you?"

Her brows furrow again. "You are not comparing sex to snuggling, are you?"

"To you, sex is…"

"It's emotional and opens me to a vulnerability I'm not ready to show."

"That's how I feel about cuddling and sleeping. I did it once eleven years ago, and it ended in tragedy. After that day, I told myself I'd never do it again, along with never getting involved in a relationship. I wouldn't allow myself to be left open like that."

She rests her shoulder against the couch cushion, moving her body closer to my hand. "What happened eleven years ago that made you change your life entirely?"

"There was a girl, Carrie. She was twenty, and we were in college. She was beautiful, funny, and so full of life. I was crazy about her." I keep my eyes on Arlo as I talk, trying to get the words out no matter how painful the memories are. "We got into a car accident, and she died. I was a mess for years. It took therapy and a lot of self-care before I could forgive myself. But I knew I never wanted to experience that pain again. To do that, I couldn't and wouldn't allow myself to have any possibility of falling in love."

She lifts her arm, placing her hand on my bicep. “I’m sorry, Mello.”

“Thanks, babe. It was a long time ago. But sometimes, I can still hear her laughter, and I know I’m the reason no one else will ever hear it again.”

“It was an accident, sweetie,” she says, giving me a sad smile.

“I know, but since I was driving, I’ll always question what I could’ve done differently to keep her alive.”

“That’ll only lead to sadness.”

“I know that too. Headed down that path for a long time, finding nothing at the end but a heaviness I couldn’t shake.”

Her fingers tighten on my muscle. “You don’t seem to be on that path anymore, though. You seem really happy.”

“I never stay still for long, Arlo. Stillness has always led me astray.”

“But you asked Lily to help you settle down, didn’t you? When she told me about it, I volunteered to help. In all honesty, I wanted to see you again.” She pauses, and we stare at each other for a second before she continues. “It’s the least I could do to pay you back, and the tattoo was a bonus.”

“I thought you came for my mad ink skills.” I dip my eyes to her ribs and my mark before going back to her face. “It is a work of beauty, just like the girl wearing it.”

“Does that shit work on people?” she asks with a smile.

“Usually.”

She laughs. “Women are too easy.”

“That they are.”

“And about us?”

“I’m thirty-one now and getting older. At first, it was a game to placate my cousin, but now…”

“Now what?”

I shrug. “I’m so fucking drawn to you, I think I’m going crazy.”

“I’m just the new girl and unconquered.”

“That’s not true. It’s something else. Something I can’t explain.”

“It’ll wear off.”

“A woman like you doesn’t wear off, Arlo.”

“We do…very easily, I can assure you.” She sighs, but there’s a pain behind the harshness of her exhale.

“If that were true, I wouldn’t have left the bar tonight alone. In my entire life, that has *never* happened to me. Never. Not even when I was seeing Carrie—we had an open relationship, before you think I was cheating on her. I never cheated because I was never exclusive.”

She blinks, her lips parted. “You’ve never been exclusive? Never?”

“Never.”

"You're so weird," she tells me, her fingers wandering aimlessly across the ink on my upper arm.

"I always thought people who were monogamous were the weird ones."

She laughs, and it's a glorious sound. "And now?"

"Still fucking weird." I shrug. "I can't change who I was. There's no taking back my past, Arlo, but I can change my future."

"We're the masters of our own destiny," she says softly.

"That we are, sweetheart. I should go," I tell her.

"I don't want you to go," she says softly, not moving her eyes away from mine.

"What do you want, Arlo?"

"You," she whispers.

I reach up, placing my hand on her cheek. "Then kiss me," I challenge her, sweeping my thumb across her lower lip.

She doesn't hesitate in putting her mouth on mine. Her lips are soft, full, and absolute perfection as she leans into me and slides her arms over my shoulders. I snake my arm around her middle, pulling her closer until our bodies are pressed together and our mouths are completely fused.

Everything about this moment feels right. The weight of her in my arms, the warmth of her skin pressed against me, the taste of her lips on mine. I could lose myself in her and do it easily.

I tear my mouth away from hers, knowing how hard it'll be for me to stop if I kiss her too long.

"Do you know how crazy you sound?"

"I do," I mutter, tilting my face upward. "God how I do."

"You spent a few hours talking with me, and you saw the light?"

"Tell me you don't feel the same or tell me that this is only a friend helping a friend fix someone, and I'll leave you alone before you have the chance to…"

She pulls me back down onto the couch, holding my hand. "To what?"

"To destroy me."

She leans forward, crawling across the couch, closing the space between us. My breath hitches, and there's an ache deep in my chest as I keep my eyes locked on hers. Arlo's in my lap, wrapping her arms around my neck before I can process what's happening.

I stare into her green eyes, too scared to move. "What are you doing?" I ask, my voice deep with need.

Her face is so close, I can feel the warmth of her breath. "Showing you how I feel."

She settles her weight in my lap, pressing against my dick, which is already pissed at me. "Arlo," I whisper, moving my hands to her back to hold her. "Maybe we…"

She puts her finger to my lips. "Shh, Mello. Stop talking," she whispers.

I can't take my eyes off her as she moves forward, pressing her lips to mine. The soft warmth of her mouth feels right against mine, and I flatten my hands, pulling her closer.

The kiss is light at first, me testing the waters and her seemingly unsure. But within seconds, her lips part and her tongue sweeps across my lip, letting me know she's not wavering at all. I open to her, letting her take the lead, not wanting her to regret this moment.

Her fingers twist in my hair as she shifts her bottom against my dick before a moan escapes her lips. I'm panting, inhaling everything she's giving me, feeling light-headed from the contact.

I press her back into the couch and cover her with my body, careful not to touch her ribs. "I could do this all night," I murmur against her lips.

"Me too," she breathes.

And I do.

I kiss her until I can't keep my eyes open anymore. Pulling her against my side, I easily drift off to sleep for only the second time in the last eleven years.

14

THE NEXT MORNING, ARLO'S BODY IS PLASTERED against mine with her arm slung over my chest, and I'm surprisingly okay with it.

"Morning," I whisper, sliding my hand down the soft skin of her arm, seeing her eyes open too.

"Hey," she says, tipping her head back. "You're still here."

"I am." I smile.

"We slept so late. I don't remember the last time I slept this long."

"What time is it?"

"Ten."

"Ten?" I ask, shocked.

"Yeah."

"Fuck," I groan, wishing I could stay like this all day. But it's Sunday, and that means family.

If I didn't show up at my grandparents' house, I'd be in trouble with my grandmother first and be barraged with questions from everyone else.

Sundays are sacred, and unless you have a good excuse, your ass always shows, and you are on time too. Nonna doesn't play around with tardiness, and neither do my parents.

"I can't stay long. I have family shit today."

She lifts up on her elbow, stroking my chest with her other hand. "It's okay. I have work to do."

"Lily said you're a writer. What do you write?"

"Articles mostly, but I'm working on a novel."

"I have a cousin in Chicago who's a writer. You're from Chicago, right?"

"Yeah, and I know all about Bianca. I love her work."

I blink. "You know who she is?"

Arlo slaps my chest playfully. "Carmello, she's super popular. I don't know anyone who reads romance and doesn't know who Bianca is. She's that big, and Lily told me about her too."

"Well, damn. I didn't know. To me, she's just another cousin."

Arlo snuggles back into my side. "I've spoken with Bianca, actually. She's the one who gave me the courage to chase my dream of publishing a novel."

I move my hand to her lower back, tracing her spine

with my fingertips. “Always chase your dreams, babe. Always.”

“Is Inked your dream?” she asks from my chest.

“It always was. I could’ve gone to work with my dad, but my idea of a good time doesn’t involve sitting for twelve hours on a stakeout or getting my ass shot at by a cheating husband.”

Her hand stops moving on my chest. “What?”

“My dad and uncle own a security slash private investigation company. They’ve had a wild ride at times, but it’s more boring than exciting most days. I had two paths to choose from…Inked or ALFA. I chose Inked and haven’t regretted that decision a single day.”

“I can see that. Everyone seems to love one another there.”

“We do. My family is insane and all up in one another’s business, but I couldn’t imagine being anywhere else. You know?”

“Yeah,” she whispers. “It must be nice to be surrounded by people who want to be around you.”

“And your people?” I ask her.

She tenses in my arms. “I don’t want to bring this conversation down, Mello.” She sighs. “What time do you have to leave?”

I shift my body, moving myself upward until my back is flush against the pillows, and I bring her with me. “I know we barely know each other, and you can totally tell me to fuck off, but don't worry about bringing me down. I want to know who you are, where you come from, and who made you this strong, kick-ass chick next to me."

Arlo sits up, laying her legs across mine, and twists her fingers together. "I don't have people, Mello. It's just me."

I place my hands on her legs, giving her thigh a squeeze. "No one?"

"No one," she repeats, gazing down at her hands. "I was adopted at birth, and then my parents died when I was eight. After that, I went into foster care, bouncing around from house to house, until I was eighteen and was turned out."

I furrow my brows, my fingers tightening. "Turned out?"

"When you're eighteen, you get emancipated and basically kicked to the curb to fend for yourself. I got lucky, though, when an agent saw me on the beach, offering me a career in modeling, which gave me the ability to support myself with a roof over my head and food in my belly. Otherwise, I don't know where I'd be."

"Jesus," I mutter, hating to think of her at a young age with no one and nothing. "That's awful, Arlo."

She shrugs and finally looks at me with those striking green eyes. "I didn't know any different. I mean, I know it's not how it is for every kid, but I was surrounded by other foster kids, and it's the reality for a lot of us. No one wants to adopt an older child when there are cute babies in need of a home without all the emotional baggage."

I seriously can't imagine. I've been blessed with two loving parents and a giant family my entire life. Then there's Rocco, my twin. Not a day has passed when I don't have someone to turn to or lean on when shit gets rough.

"And your birth parents…did you ever look for them?"

"I never have. I didn't see the point. They didn't want me then, and the last thing I wanted to do was make them feel guilty about giving me up only to have a shit life."

"But you have a good life now," I tell her, looking around her fancy place. "A pretty impressive life."

She looks around too, seeing what I see, and smiles. "I have the life I created, and I don't think letting someone else into that life would be wise, especially if I wasn't wanted in the first place."

I grab her hands, wrapping my fingers around hers. "Maybe you were wanted, but they weren't able to take care of you or were too young."

She gives me a sorrowful smile. "Maybe, but I'm perfectly content leaving the past in the past. It's easier for me that way."

“I can understand, sugar. I don’t know what I would do in your circumstances.”

“You’re kind of sweet.”

“Only kind of?” I tease her, trying to lighten the mood.

“You’re mostly an asshole with a little sweet mixed in.”

“You nailed me. Can’t argue with the truth, babe.” There’s silence for a few seconds before I say, “Thank you for sharing that with me.”

She snuggles into my side, placing her hand back against my chest, right over my heart. “You opened up to me last night, so it was only fair that I opened up to you.”

“I needed you to understand why I do fucked-up shit. It’s different. You didn’t need to open up to me.”

“I need you to understand why I’m fucked up too,” she whispers against my bare chest.

“I don’t think you’re fucked up.”

She tips her head back again, staring up at me. “How many people do you know my age who are single and not sleeping around, Mello?”

I grimace, getting her point. “Just you, babe.”

“See. That’s fucked up.”

“That’s sweet,” I correct her. “Nothing fucked up about it.”

She moves her eyes away from me, pointing them

down the length of my body. "I clearly have trust and intimacy issues, or else I'd be different."

"I don't want different."

"Sure," she mutters.

"I've had different, Arlo, and it's not all it's cracked up to be."

"I'm sure every thirty-one-year-old man dreams of dating a woman who doesn't want to have sex with him."

"You don't want to have sex with me?"

She stares up at me, blinking. "I mean…"

"And every thirty-one-year-old man wants a woman just like you…at least for their wife. Trust me on that one."

"That's me. Every man's fantasy."

"You really are, sugar. You don't know the preciousness of what you hold."

"It's typically about conquest for them. They think they're going to be the one to get the golden ticket, and when they don't…they're pissed. So, just so we're clear, you're not getting my V-card."

"Got it," I tell her.

"Not unless we're married," she adds.

"Got that too. One thing I will never do is pressure you. If I wanted easy, empty pussy, I wouldn't be here."

"You could have good pussy that isn't me. There are women out there who are more suited to your tastes and needs."

"Arlo," I say when she turns her head back down. "Look at me, babe." A second later, she does, giving me her green eyes. "If I wanted easy, I'd have easy. But I want Arlo and whatever comes with her. We've spent two nights on the couch together, and you know what?"

"What?" she whispers, her eyes locked with mine and not blinking.

I slide my hand against her cheek, cradling her face in my palm. "They were the two best nights I've had in a long time."

She smiles, curling into my grip. "Thank you for that, even if it was a lie."

"No lie, Arlo. I'm being one hundred percent honest with you."

"Okay," she mumbles. "Whatever you say."

"Listen, I don't lie. It's not me. I'll always be honest with you. It's the most important thing I have with those closest to me. We love one another deeply, but we're also honest. And sometimes it's brutal."

"So, you're going to be mean?" she asks.

"No, Arlo. I'll never be mean to you. I don't think I could be, but just like I told you about the chick at the bar…that was brutal and not so pretty, but it was honest as fuck."

"I don't know if I want *that* much honesty," she says with a small laugh. "There is such a thing as too much."

"Got it," I tell her. "Now, do you have to work today, or do you want to come to my grandma's?"

Her eyes widen. "You'd want me to go with you?"

I nod. "Why not? Everybody has to eat, and she makes the best sauce in the world."

"That's kind of a big deal. Your cousins have told me about the famous Sunday dinners."

"It's not that big of a deal, babe. Lily, Gigi, Tamara, and my other cousins will be there. We can hang by the pool and have some great food. Why should you sit here all day by yourself, slaving away at the keyboard, when you could be with me, laughing and eating the best pasta in town?"

She doesn't speak for a second as her eyes move across my face, and I can see the wheels inside her pretty head spinning around. "I don't know."

"Just come. Please. I can't walk out your door after an amazing night like that and know you're here alone."

"Oh, goody. I'm suddenly a charity case," she says and sighs. "This is why I don't tell people about my past."

"You're not a charity case, silly woman, you're my girl, and I refuse to leave you here. So, get your fine ass up, shower, put on a shirt that covers your stomach, and get ready to eat more than you've eaten in your entire life."

"You sure?" she asks.

"Wouldn't ask if I weren't."

"What time do you have to be there?"

"One."

"Shit!" she screeches, jumping up off me and away from the couch. "That's not much time."

"It's casual, Ar. Just throw on whatever."

"Casual?" She looks horrified. "A dinner with an entire family is never casual."

"Mine is," I tell her, moving to sit up and swinging my legs off the couch. "Totally casual and, anyway, you're beautiful."

"Are you sure they wouldn't feel weird with me there?"

"Hold on. Lemme ask." I'm only placating her, making sure she's comfortable. "I'll send out a text."

"Okay." She shifts her weight back and forth between her feet. "Do that."

Me: Everyone okay with Arlo coming to dinner at Gram's today?

I hand her the phone as I stalk into the kitchen, needing a bottle of water.

"Why did you give this to me?" she asks, following right behind with the phone in her hand.

"Just watch," I tell her, opening the fridge.

The phone starts to ping a few seconds later, and I walk back to her, looking over her shoulder.

Lily: OMG. For real?

Gigi: Fuck yeah.

Pike: Oh boy.

Mammoth: The first step is accepting the inevitable.

"What's that mean?" she asks me as soon as she sees Mammoth's text.

"He's a little out there," I lie, not wanting her to know he thinks we're destined to be together.

Tamara: We could use another woman around the table.

Rocco: Mom's going to love this.

Arlo's eyes come to mine. "Should I worry about your mom?"

I shake my head and laugh. "No, sugar. My mother is going to love you."

"Oh. Okay."

"She's different and totally badass in her own way. Just go along with whatever she says, and you'll be fine."

"Um," she mumbles, pulling the corner of her lip in between her teeth.

I place my hand over hers before taking the phone back. "It'll be fine. Go get ready because nothing makes my grandma madder than being late."

Arlo pops up on her toes, planting a big kiss on my lips. "Thanks, Mello."

"For what?" I ask, resisting the urge to pull her into my arms for more.

"For including me."

"Always," I reply, hoping I can keep the promise. "Now, go."

She scurries away, those tight yoga pants doing

nothing to help the morning wood I've been sporting since my eyes opened.

My hand and I are about to be best friends again, and I'm not sure how I feel about that.

But when I hear Arlo's laughter, I know the best things lie before me and not in the past.

15

ROCCO AND MY MOTHER ARE ON THE FRONT PORCH, waiting for us when we pull in. They're whispering, watching us as we weave our way through the two rows of cars filling the driveway.

"Hey," I say, giving my brother a chin lift.

"Hey," he replies with a smirk and the same chin lift.

My mother comes down the two steps and meets us on the sidewalk. "I'm Izzy, Rocco and Mello's mom."

Arlo smiles, coming to a stop, not knowing my mom is a hugger and is about to pull her in. "It's nice to meet you. I'm Arlo King."

Ma holds out her arms, motioning for Arlo to move forward. "We hug in this family, dear."

Arlo looks at me, and I nod, before she looks back at

my mom. “Okay,” she whispers, stepping quickly into my mother’s embrace.

“Another girl. The tide is turning in our favor.”

Rocco shrugs at Arlo, who’s probably giving him a confused face. “She’s obsessed with adding females to the family.”

Ma pulls back, her hands still on Arlo’s arms. “I wanted girls, but instead, I was given three pain-in-the-ass boys.”

“You love us, though,” Rocco says.

“Yeah. I do, but I would’ve loved to have a wee one to put a dress on and shop with.”

“Well, you do it with Rebel, Liv, and Adaline now, Ma.”

“True,” Ma says, smiling at Arlo as she finally releases her. “You can totally shop with us too. We go once a week and have lunch.”

“Maybe,” Arlo says softly, moving away from my mother and coming back to my side.

“Think about it.”

“I will.”

“Mello, bring her in and make sure to introduce her to everyone. Don’t do what your brother did with Rebel. Don’t be lazy.”

“I won’t be,” I promise her. “She’ll meet everyone.”

“Good.” Ma brushes her long brown hair over her shoulder, looking just as beautiful as she did when I was younger. "Welcome to the group, Arlo. Make yourself at home and eat a lot. It'll make my mom happy."

"Yes, ma'am."

Rocco shakes his head, and I brace for my mother's reaction, knowing she's always hated that word.

"Never ma'am. Izzy, Isabella, or Mom."

"Got it, Izzy." Arlo nods slowly. "Sorry."

"Don't be sorry. I just never felt like a ma'am."

"Ma, it's the South, for shit's sake. You make us call other women ma'am," Rocco reminds her.

Ma smiles, turning to my brother. "It's respectful, and that always makes me feel younger."

"You're weird," he replies.

"A woman has to keep any edge she has."

I roll my eyes. "Can we go in?"

Ma steps to the side, motioning for us to move.

"Thanks," I say, giving her a wink and getting one in return.

I seriously have the world's best mother. She's a total badass. She had to be in order to raise three crazy-as-hell boys who were hell-bent on trying to end their lives with insane antics at a young age. Then there's my father, who isn't easy by any stretch of the imagination. Somehow, she managed not to go insane over the last thirty-plus years, instead handling us with love and grace.

"Ready?" I ask Arlo as we step inside.

"Yeah. I think so," she says, but she's lost some of the color in her face, clearly nervous.

"They're going to love you, and anyway, they're busy with their own Sunday routines. They'll barely pay any attention to you." I keep her at my side, pressing against her lower back to move her forward.

I eat those words as soon as we leave the foyer and hit the back of the house, where the kitchen and living room are.

Every member of my family is silent, staring at us with goofy smiles.

"Um," Arlo whispers.

"Hi," I say, but it comes out more like a question.

My gram steps between us and them. "Hi, sweetie. Don't mind the nosy rosies. They're harmless, and they're staring at Carmello, not you."

"Okay," Arlo says, moving into my side.

"Hey, Gram."

"Baby," she whispers, reaching up to touch my face, followed by pressing her lips to my cheek. "You look happy."

"I am happy."

"Good," she says, her face soft and sweet. "That's all a grandmother wants to hear."

"I'm Gram," she says to Arlo. "You can call me Gram, Nonna, or Grandma. I refuse to answer to anything else at my age and when we're with family."

"But I'm not family," Arlo replies, and I brace

myself again, knowing my family is a pain in the dick about this shit.

"If Mello brought you here, you are. And anyway, anyone who walks through my front door becomes an honorary member. You're in now for as long as you want. Now, come here and give me a hug."

Arlo looks at me, and I give her a little shove forward. There's no getting away from the formalities of this family, no matter who the person is.

"So pretty," Gram says, wrapping Arlo in her arms. "My grandson did good."

"Lily set us up," I tell my grandma for no reason at all.

Gram smiles as she lets go of Arlo. "Then this one's a good girl, too. None of that trash I know he's been seen around town with for years."

My face heats, and I can't look her in the eyes. "That's not true."

"Don't lie to me, Carmello. Small towns make word travel fast and wide. I hear things, and you tend to be the favorite topic of the worst gossips."

"Sorry, Gram," is all I can say. "I'll do better."

"Just be you."

"I always am."

"Lord, how I know. Now, go introduce your girl to everyone."

Arlo is about to open her mouth, but I jump in and say, "Will do, Gram."

"Lovely to meet you, Arlo. Please don't leave here hungry."

Arlo smiles. "Based on the smell, I don't think that will be an issue."

"Need to fatten you up. No babies as long as you're that skinny."

"What?" Arlo's eyes widen.

"Nothing, sweetie," Gram says before wandering away.

The others are still relatively quiet, whispering among themselves, probably placing bets on how long my *relationship* will last. Can't say I blame them. I've never settled down, and before Arlo, I never planned to either.

"Arlo, this is my nosy-as-hell family." I wave my arm out, motioning toward the entire group.

They all smile in unison, looking creepy as fuck.

"I don't know what's wrong with them," I whisper to her. "It's like they've all lost their minds."

"No, son. Seeing you here with Arlo is like looking into the sky and seeing God himself descending through the clouds. Two things we never anticipated experiencing in our lifetimes," my grandpa says, stepping through the group.

I shake my head, trying to hold back my laughter at their stupidity. "That's ridiculous."

Grandpa places his hand on my shoulder and gives me a wink. "The truth sometimes is, but you made us think it was never going to happen." He then moves his eyes to Arlo. "Hello, sweet girl. Welcome to our home."

"Thank you," Arlo replies.

"These are my kids, grandkids, and great-grandkids. If they say anything crazy, ignore them. They're not all right in the head because we spoiled them."

"Pop, stop lying," my uncle Joe says. "You're hardly normal, so stop acting like you are." My uncle lifts his hand in greeting to Arlo. "I'm his uncle Joe, Gigi's father."

Arlo smiles, her cheeks turning pink. "It's nice to meet you."

"You have your hands full with this one," Uncle Joe says.

Her smile widens as she looks at me and then back to him. "I'm well aware."

"Nothing about him has been easy since he was born," Uncle Joe says.

"Can we not kick up the last thirty years just this second?" I ask him, knowing my family has been salivating for this moment. "Save it for next time."

Uncle Joe raises an eyebrow. "Sure, kid. I got a lifetime, and I'm a patient man."

"That shit is the truth," my mom mutters.

"I'm going to run down the line. Everyone keep gawking like weirdos until I say your name and then peel your ass away and go back to acting as normal as you possibly can."

Dad laughs in the background, keeping watch over the family, and my mom is at his side, snuggled against him.

I go down the line, starting from left to right, and Arlo's body is completely still. I know it's a lot to take in, and she'll never remember who they are, but I want them to go back to acting semi-normal in front of her, or else she'll never come over again.

When I'm finally done, they do as I asked, peeling off and going back to their usual places. The older adults head to the living room, some of the women, especially my cousins, head to the lanai, and the younger people move toward the den. The people who can cook go to the kitchen to finish prepping dinner, which is no easy feat with this many people.

The only person who doesn't move is my father. He takes a few steps forward, stopping right in front of us. "I'm James, Carmello's dad."

"Hi," she squeaks, tipping her head back to make eye contact.

He gives her a genuine smile. "They're a lot, but don't worry, Arlo. Once you're in, no one will love you more deeply than this family."

Arlo's mouth opens and closes, but nothing comes out.

Dad looks at me and then back to her. "You okay?"

"Great. Great," she replies, finding her words, but she hasn't taken her eyes off him. "I'm sorry. I'm just totally dumb struck by how much your boys look like you. I mean, Mrs. Caldo is beautiful, but you're… you're…"

"Fuck me," I mutter.

Her gaze swings to me. "You come from good genes, Mello. That's all. You have to remember, I have no idea what my parents look like. I can see where you get your eyes, your nose, your jaw. I don't have that, and it always throws me off when I see people with their parents. You and your two brothers all look more like your dad—with tiny splashes of your mom too, of course."

"My genes are stronger, but that's not surprising," Dad says proudly.

"Even your genes are bossy, Pop."

Dad's smile is genuine. "Arlo, what did you mean about your parents? Were you adopted?"

"I was right after I was born."

"And you didn't ask your parents about them?"

Her gaze dips to the floor. "They died when I was eight."

Dad's face changes, and he's no longer smiling. "And what happened to you?"

"Foster care," Arlo whispers. "And after I turned eighteen, I never bothered looking for them."

"I'm sorry," he says to her. "If you ever want to look for them, you come see me and I'll do my best to find them."

"Thank you, Mr. Caldo."

"James," he corrects her. "And no problem. My door is always open to you."

"You probably won't hear from me. They haven't looked for me, so I don't know why I'd look for them."

Dad reaches out and takes Arlo's hands in his. "You don't know that. When kids enter foster care, it's easy for records and files to be lost or mislabeled. They may have looked but come up with nothing but dead ends."

Her shoulders slump, but she does her best to recover, giving him a smile. "I'll think about it."

"Good. Now, I'm going to go watch the game. You two enjoy yourself." Dad dips his chin and gives my shoulder a tight squeeze.

"Thanks, Pop."

"I can't believe you're related to all these people," Arlo tells me once my dad stalks off. "I will never remember their names."

My heart aches for her because I know she has no one except biological parents she's never met. I squeeze her hand and smile. "Every single one, and I know I'm lucky as shit. They're a lot to take in. Don't worry about remembering their names. Use Mr. or Mrs. Gallo when in doubt, and ninety-five percent of the time, you'll be right."

"Can we go over some of them again? I really pride myself on remembering names and details."

"We can do whatever you want," I tell her, liking the

idea that she wants to take the time to get to know my family.

"Who's he again?" she asks, ticking her head directly across the room.

"That's my cousin Morgan. His mom, Aunt Fran, and my grandpa are brother and sister. His wife's name is Race, and he works with my dad at ALFA."

"And Fran is married to Dog?"

I shake my head. "She's married to Bear."

"Ahh. Right. Bear," she repeats.

"Bear is one of my uncle Joe's oldest friends."

She looks at me funny. "So, his good friend married his aunt?"

I grimace. "When you put it that way, it sounds gross."

"I'm just getting the logistics down. I'm not making any judgments."

"That's like me marrying one of my aunt's friends, which is just weird."

Arlo pats my hand. "Don't think about it."

"I'm trying not to," I mutter with a shiver.

"And him?" she asks, changing the subject.

"Bear's son, Ret."

"And the two women at his side?"

"One is his wife, and the other is their…"

"Got it," she says quickly, not letting me finish. "I can figure that one out."

"Alese and Nya are their names. They've been together as long as I've been alive."

"It looks like it works for them."

"They have two sons a little younger than me. Both are in the military somewhere in the world, but their location is secret. Ret is former military, and the boys took after him."

"Interesting," she whispers. "He looks former military."

"He works at ALFA with my dad too."

"So, you weren't kidding about everyone either working at ALFA or Inked, were you?"

"Told ya, babe. Tamara and Mammoth have their own business, but you've been there. And Lily's mom owns a clinic, but other than that…pretty much."

"That's amazing. Your family is really interesting."

"I guess they are," I tell her.

"Hey," Lily says, locking her arm with Arlo's before we have a chance to take a step. "The girls want you to come outside and hang out."

Arlo looks at me. "You mind?"

"No, sugar. You go with Lily. I'll deal with my mom."

"I should stay with you," she replies.

I shake my head. "Go, babe. Hang out with the ladies. I'm sure they want all the juicy details. It's like gossip central out there."

"Shut up," Lily snaps. "We don't gossip. We share

the truth and talk about the guys and their shit-tastic behavior. Anyway, she was mine first."

"Technically, she wasn't," I tease, but before I can say anything more, Lily pulls Arlo outside, closing the door behind them and heading right toward the table with Gigi, Tamara, Rebel, and Jo.

"Man, your ears are going to be on fire, brother," Trace says, coming to stand next to me and staring out the sliding glass door. "How you got such a fine piece of ass…I'll never know."

"She's not a piece of ass. Watch your mouth."

"Touchy fucker, aren't you?"

I turn my head, glaring at my younger, cockier brother. "Just keep her name off your tongue."

He smiles. "I like this caveman side of you. It's kind of full of anger just below the surface, which is a nice change."

"Anger is never a good look," I tell him.

He smirks. "Nah. It suits you along with the territorial alpha trait from Dad you're letting loose."

I sigh, pinching the bridge of my nose. "Why are you busting my balls, Trace?"

"Because I can," he says and then walks away.

"Don't listen to that little shit," Aunt Fran says, coming to stand at my side, clearly eavesdropping. "He's jealous, baby. It looks like you may have finally gotten your head out of your ass and found yourself a good girl." She hooks her arm through mine, putting her head against my bicep. "Now, don't fuck it up."

I peer down at her salt-and-pepper hair. "And how do I make sure I don't do that, Auntie?"

"Always make her feel like the most important thing in the world and never take whatever piece of herself she gives you for granted. Even the strongest person wants someone in their corner, having their back, and showering them with love. She's no different. A good woman is worth the extra effort and sometimes requires more attention and understanding. I know you two are new to each other, but don't use that as an excuse to be lazy."

"Got it, Auntie. Thanks."

"And when all else fails, use what the good Lord gave you to dickmatize her." I give her a pained look.

"Dickmatize," she repeats with a quick nod. "Bear dickmatized me, and I didn't even really like him then."

"Woman, you're lying. You always liked me," he says from a few feet away, also eavesdropping. "But I did give you the good dick, so I won't disagree with the dickmatizing."

My stomach rolls because I don't want to talk about sex or dicks with Aunt Fran and Uncle Bear. "Thanks for the great advice," I tell her and him, although he hasn't added much to the conversation.

"The way to a woman's heart isn't just by listening to them talk and giving them attention. You got to give them the good dick and lots of orgasms. It's amazing how many assholes can't find a clit to save their own life. Orgasms make you memorable."

I look around, hoping someone's nearby to save me from this awkward and uncomfortable conversation with my aunt and uncle, but there's no one. "I'll remember this conversation for the rest of my life," I grumble.

Bear laughs. "Just keeping shit real."

"And awkward," I whisper.

Aunt Fran laughs, patting my stomach. "You've had it easy far too long, Carmello. The real test of a man is when he has it hard, and we're about to see what you're really made of, baby. Fight the good fight."

"Have you two dipped into the wine early today?" I ask her.

She tips her head back and laughs. "I won't lie. I've had two glasses, but you know I never have a filter even when I'm one hundred percent sober."

"I like your mouth most of all, baby," Bear tells her.

I somehow hold in the vomit that's about to crawl up my throat. There's a difference when it comes to talking about sex with my cousins and the elders of the family. I know they've had sex or else none of us would be here, but it's not something I really let myself soak in or put much thought into because it's just too much. "I think Arlo needs me outside."

"Sure, baby," Aunt Fran says, finally moving toward

her husband. "You go get that girl, and don't let her go without a fight. Dickmatize her."

"Dickmatize. Got it," I say, walking toward the sliding glass doors, thankful that conversation is over.

I've dickmatized more than a few women over the years. None of them I wanted, but they got a taste and wanted more. But how am I going to dickmatize Arlo without having sex?

Orgasms. Lots of orgasms.

16

"You locked that shit down quick," Pike says as I sit down at the table on the lanai after dinner. "Quicker than I thought possible."

Gigi smiles as her gaze moves to Arlo and Lily huddled together, talking on the other side of the patio. "Even a man as experienced as Carmello can pull his head out of his ass eventually."

"Thanks," I mumble sarcastically, turning a beer bottle in my hand, keeping my gaze pinned on the ladies.

"I'm proud of you. Today was a big step," she adds. "You've never brought anyone here, so that says a lot about how you feel and your intentions."

"We're new, Gigi. I'm not putting a ring on her finger or anything."

"Not soon, at least," Gigi replies.

"One family dinner doesn't mean marriage."

"No," she says, shaking her head. "It doesn't, but it's a step in the right direction. You've never brought any of your other bimbos here, and I know Arlo and she's absolutely perfect for you."

Tamara rolls her eyes. "Have you found your way into Arlo's pants yet, Mello?"

"No," I snap, lifting the beer to my lips, feeling dirty talking about Arlo without her around. "And it's none of your business."

Tamara sits up straighter with a smile on her lips. "Ooh. I like this side of you. You finally sound like your father."

I growl, and Tamara laughs along with Mammoth, Pike, and Gigi. Jett is weirdly quiet, busy typing on his phone.

"Why are you silent?" I ask him from across the table.

He shrugs. "I don't know, man. I really like Arlo and…"

"You think I'm playing a game?"

He pushes his sunglasses up on his head, finally giving me his eyes. "I think you are. One taste and you're going to be out the door so fucking fast, you won't look back. You're going to really hurt that girl, and she doesn't deserve your kind of bullshit."

"That's rich. Is the pot calling the kettle black?"

His lip snarls. "Lily and I had history, and I wasn't

pretending with your cousin, nor were we forced together. I knew once I crossed that bridge, there was no turning back. Our families were too intertwined for me to walk out of her life. I worry Arlo will want to tell you to fuck off but won't be able to do it."

"She's had no problem so far," I reassure him.

"Do you know about her past? About how she was brought up?"

I nod. "She told me."

"Then you know she's never had a family like this." He waves his arms around the lanai and toward the house. "This is something someone like her would always dream of having, and now you've shown it to her. Are you trying to reel her in, using what you know about her past against her?"

I touch my hand to my chest, trying to stop myself from reaching across the table to punch him square in the face. "I'm not using anything against her, asshole. She was going to sit at home by herself today. Should I have just left her instead? I swear to God, it doesn't matter what I do. You guys will question my motives. If I'd left her, you would've called me out for being uncaring." Those words I say to everyone around the table and not just to Jett. "And by bringing her here, I'm being accused of using my secret family weapon to get in the woman's panties."

"Fair enough," Mammoth says. "We can't judge

what's in your heart. We've all known Arlo for a while, and we're looking out for her."

"What about me?" I ask.

Mammoth's forehead crinkles. "What about you?"

"Who's going to look out for me?"

Everyone laughs.

"I'm being serious."

Pike runs his hand down his face. "Brother, you're like a rock. No one can crack you."

"You all claim to know Arlo so well. You don't think she has the power to destroy me just as much as I have the ability to ruin her?"

Mammoth leans back and grabs Tamara's hand. "I get what you're saying. I do, man. Tamara could've wiped me out if she would've left me. Everyone thinks we're made of granite, but we have the ability to crack too. I believe your intentions are true with Arlo, but I'm telling you right now, you yank that girl's chain for fun, and I'm going to bust your nose, ruining your pretty face forever."

I lift my hands, giving him my palms. "I'm not looking for more than she's willing to give."

"Hey." Arlo's voice comes from behind me before her hand lands on my shoulder. "Everything okay?"

I tip my head back, smiling up at her. "Perfect. You two done?"

"Yep," Lily answers for her. "Just a quick girl chat."

"Nothing important," Arlo tells me, moving into the chair next to me. "You okay?"

"Couldn't be better," I reply.

"You want to come over tonight? We'll light a fire, have a few drinks, and watch the meteor shower," Lily asks, but she is looking at Arlo when she speaks. "It's supposed to be amazing."

"I should really work tonight." Arlo glances my way and smiles. "I was supposed to write all afternoon, but—"

"Are you on a deadline?" Lily asks before Arlo can finish the statement.

"Sort of, but I'm always on a deadline."

"Maybe another night," Lily replies, but I can hear the disappointment in her voice.

"We'll come," Gigi tells Lily.

"Us too," Tamara adds.

"Wouldn't miss it," Jo says. "Nick bought a telescope."

My gaze moves to my cousin, shocked that he's that into the stars. "You bought a telescope?"

He gives me the middle finger. "My girl likes stargazing, and whatever she likes, I'm going to make it happen, even if I have to build her a telescope in the backyard like we're an extension of NASA."

"Weirdo," I mutter.

"Arlo, you like looking at the stars?"

She nods. "There's a beauty in the celestial heavens. A majesty that can't be recreated."

"Then come," Lily tells her. "You can write tomorrow."

Arlo peers over at me, and I know she's wanting to hear what my plans are. And just like my cousin Nick, I'd do just about anything she wanted, even if it means staring up at the sky all night. "I'll go if you're going to be there."

"Another night off isn't going to kill me. I'll just have to write twice as much tomorrow."

"What are you working on now?" Gigi asks.

"The side project I've been talking to you guys about for a while."

It really hits me then that they've all been friends for some time, and I never knew it. They hid Arlo from me —rightfully so, too.

"That's exciting," Gigi says. "You're going to do amazing."

"What is it?" I ask, feeling stupid for not knowing.

"I'm writing a book about a teenager trying to survive the foster care system."

"Is it nonfiction?" I ask her, reaching out to cover her hand with mine as it lies flat on her chair's armrest.

She shakes her head. "It's fiction, but there's a sprinkling of my real life in there. Things I haven't discussed with anyone, but it's been almost therapeutic getting it all down on paper."

"Can I read it?" I ask, squeezing her fingers.

"Not yet. It's not ready."

"But when it's ready…"

"Maybe." She smiles. "My agent may say it's trash, and no one may want to buy it. It may never see the light of day."

"That's harsh. I can't imagine putting myself out there and getting rejected after all that hard work."

Arlo gives me a sad smile. "It's part of the business. You have to be willing to be turned down a lot, or else you'll never make it in this industry."

"Carmello's never dealt with much rejection in his life," Tamara teases.

"And what rejection have you dealt with, Tam? You were the female version of me."

She laughs. "I was, wasn't I?"

I nod. "You weren't an angel, waiting around for your dream man to fall into your lap. How did you meet Mammoth anyway?" I ask, raising an eyebrow.

"I don't think I ever heard this story," Arlo says, and I know Tamara can't skate over the details since Arlo's asking instead of me.

"I was at the compound where he lived," Tamara says.

Mammoth grunts. "That asshole."

"Which asshole?" Arlo asks, looking back and forth between Mammoth and Tamara.

"I showed up at the biker compound looking for

someone else, but he was a total dick and pretended to not want me around."

"He was a fool, but thank God, or else maybe you'd be with him and not me."

Tamara scrunches her nose. "I wouldn't have waited around for him while he was inside."

"Inside?" Arlo asks, her eyebrows drawn down.

"He went to prison for a while."

Arlo's eyes widen as soon as those words are out of Tamara's mouth. "Holy shit," she whispers.

Tamara nods. "Anyway, I showed up, he ignored me, told me to turn my ass around and leave, but Morris, who's a dreamy guy in that scary kind of way, took me in and put Mammoth on me."

"No one hit on her, but I was told to babysit her for the night to make sure nothing happened to her. Because there were a lot of horny bastards around, and when her fine piece of ass walked in the door looking all cute, they all noticed. I was supposed to take her home the next day."

"You thought I looked cute?" Tamara asks him.

"Babe, told you that a million times. I knew I was going to get in your pants if you'd let me. No way I was walking away from you without getting a taste."

"Dude, that's my cousin," Nick tells Mammoth.

"She's my wife," he shoots back.

"There's always too much information sharing with this family," I add.

Arlo smiles, moving her elbow to the table and her chin to her palm. "Tell me more."

"Anyway, we kissed a little the first night."

"Wait, I thought you were going home the next day?" Arlo asks, confused.

"The compound went on lockdown." Tamara shrugs like it's no big deal, but it was a very big deal. "And we used our time wisely, keeping ourselves busy in other ways."

Mammoth gives his wife a wink, smiling at her like she's the most beautiful thing in the world. My cousin is beautiful, but she's feisty as fuck. She truly was the female version of me…wild and free.

"You have such an interesting story," Arlo tells Tamara. "You've never told me everything, but I knew you met at the compound."

"There's so much more I can tell you," Tamara offers and leans forward. "But we'll wait for the next book club."

"Wait." I lift a hand, scooting forward in my seat, keeping my hand on Arlo's. "Are you all doing book club now? I thought Lily was the only reader."

Gigi laughs. "Babe, we mostly drink and gossip, but we do read some spicy books too."

"How spicy?" I ask.

"Freakishly hot. You'd turn fifty shades of red if you read some of the shit they read," Jett tells me.

Lily's head snaps to the side to face her husband.

"You read the books?" Her mouth hangs open as she stares at him.

He nods. "Sometimes I pick them up and read a few pages. It's enough to get an idea."

"You can't tell much from a few pages."

Jett tilts his head, giving her a look. "I can tell a fuck of a lot from a few pages, baby. The shit you ladies read makes all of us look like choirboys."

Lily giggles. "It's fiction, sweetie. If you start acting like the men in the books, I'll—"

"What'll you do?" he challenges her, holding her gaze.

Arlo giggles softly. "You two are so cute together. You all are. I'm so happy Carmello took pity on me and invited me over today," she says, smiling at me, making my chest ache in a funny way.

"You're welcome back anytime, Arlo," Lily tells her. "It's not a one-time deal. Once you're in, you're in. Even after Carmello, you're welcome for dinner."

"After me?" I growl. "Who says there's an after me?"

Every single person turns their eyes toward me, looking at me like I've gone off the deep end.

"Well, a month sneaks up on you quick," Lily adds, fishing for details, probably knowing them all already.

"Don't play games," I tell Lily. "You know, don't you?"

"Know what?" Gigi asks her, elbowing Lily in the ribs.

"Mello made it official with Arlo last night after he left the bar."

Gigi's mouth falls open, and there's an audible gasp from the others at the table.

"The player is off the market?" Tamara asks me. "I mean, I assumed, but I didn't know you made it official, official."

Arlo squeezes my fingers this time. "We're exclusive, but we're going to take things slow," she tells them.

"Remember what I told you," Mammoth says, pointing a finger at me.

I give him the middle finger.

"Then you have to come over tonight to celebrate," Lily says to Arlo, setting it up so there is no way Arlo can turn her down.

I know it and so does Arlo, but being sweet, she doesn't call Lily out on her bullshit. "We'll be there," she answers for the two of us, something no one has ever done before.

And I'm oddly okay with it. Suddenly, I'm no longer a me, but a we.

17

"Do you want to come in?" Arlo asks when I walk her to her front door, always trying to be a gentleman with her.

I'd never been into chivalry. I was taught by my parents to have manners, but ninety-nine percent of the chicks I'd been with didn't give two fucks about any of that as long as they got off.

But that isn't Arlo. She wants to be courted, and chivalry is important to her—that much I gathered by listening to her speak to my cousins tonight while we watched the stars.

I rub the back of my neck, trying to find a reason to say no, but I got nothing. "I really shouldn't," I lie, not wanting the evening to end.

Arlo peers down at her feet and frowns so quick, I almost miss it. "Are you sure?"

Fuck.

I know I shouldn't go in. We've already spent more time together in the last few days than I've spent with any other woman in my life besides those I am related to. Arlo is becoming an addiction I'm not sure I'll ever be able to break.

"You can stay over," she offers.

"You want me to stay over?" I repeat, making sure my mind didn't process something other than what she said.

Oh yeah. Someone's getting some action, and that someone is me. I may not slide into home base, but staying over leads to something, and I'm down with whatever small piece of her she is willing to give.

She looks up, and those green eyes get me every time. "Well, yeah… I mean, you don't have to, but—"

I lean forward, my gaze dipping to her mouth. "No. I want to. I want to very much, sugar."

"Then come in," she says, her tongue peeking out as she speaks. "It's been a great day, and I'm not sure I'm ready for it to be over."

My brain should answer, but my dick does instead. "I'll stay," I tell her, reaching out and grabbing her hip to guide her inside. "But I'm leaving early because I have to work."

"I have to work tomorrow too, remember?"

I close the door behind me, kicking off my boots like I've done it a hundred times before. "No getting pissy with me tomorrow when I'm out of here before daylight. 'Kay?"

The last thing I need is a repeat of her attitude because I wasn't there when she woke up.

She blinks, gawking at me as we stand in the foyer. "Why so early?"

I smirk, brushing aside a few strands of hair that have fallen over her eyes. "I have to hit the gym, go home and shower, and then head to Inked. I didn't get this body by lying in bed all day."

She swallows, her eyes still trained on mine. "You're dedicated."

"I'm very dedicated when something is important to me."

She places a hand on my chest, a small smile on her lips. "Your dedication is paying off."

I've got her. I knew I had her the moment I took my shirt off at Inked and she didn't want me to put it back on. She may not be like the other women I've been with, but she knows a good thing when she sees it. And my body…is a very good thing.

"Thank you for noticing." I give her a wink.

She blushes, turning her face away from me. "I may have something that fits you to wear to bed tonight."

"I don't normally sleep with clothes on."

She snaps her face back to me, and her eyebrows are up. "Um," she mumbles. "Well…"

"I can just wear this," I reassure her, not trying to be too forward, but wishing I could lie with her naked.

She sniffs and wrinkles her nose. "You smell like a campfire."

"I hope you like the smell because it's all I got, babe. It's this or nothing."

She runs her fingers down my T-shirt, slowly moving them lower, but stopping over my abdomen. "Shirt off, then," she orders, sending a tingle down my spine and straight to my dick.

"Yes, ma'am." I smirk, reaching behind my back and slipping the soft material over my head.

She inhales as her eyes wander down my chest. "I almost forgot how pretty you are."

She almost forgot? Lies. But I won't call her out. Whatever makes her feel comfortable, including a small white lie, I am down with because it means more time with Arlo and maybe, hopefully, skin.

"Pretty?" I ask, holding my T-shirt in my hand, enjoying her slow study of my body. "I don't think anyone's called me pretty in a long time."

"You're like a work of art, Carmello."

"I'm sure you've been around guys a hell of a lot prettier than me. And you're the beautiful one, babe, not me."

It's my turn to lie. I know I'm good-looking. I'd even go as far as to call myself hot. I've never had trouble landing pussy, no matter how beautiful the girl is who is attached to it.

But Arlo is more than beautiful. I'm not even sure that's a good enough word to describe her features. She is simply stunning.

She peers up with hungry eyes, her fingers still lingering on my skin. "They were boys, but you're a man."

"Arlo, you're walking into dangerous territory. You better stop or…" I swallow, trying to keep myself under control.

I've seen that look before. Not on her face, but on a hundred other women, all wanting a piece of me. When Arlo gives me the same look, though…it's the ultimate temptation. I know once I get started, I won't want to stop.

"Or what?" she says, challenging me with an undeniable, burning desire in her gaze.

I slide my hand up her back to her neck and cradle her head. "The way you're looking at me, sugar…it's full of sin."

"I'm not an angel, Carmello," she whispers as she moves her gaze from my eyes to my lips and she drops her hands to the button on my jeans. "But if you don't want to…" she says, her voice trailing off on a whisper.

I pull her forward, taking her mouth with mine, shutting down any doubt she has about what I want or how I feel.

I've burned for her all day, wanting nothing more than to put my lips on her skin and taste the softness of her flesh. But I kept it together, behaving, when all I wanted was to do bad things to her.

She slides her hands to my back, her nails biting into the flesh just above my jeans as she kisses me back.

A moan comes from her mouth into mine, sending a jolt through my system. I walk forward, holding her in my arms and bringing her with me toward the couch we've spent two nights curled up on already.

"Bed," she murmurs against my lips and moves toward the hallway, our mouths still connected.

As soon as we get to the bedroom, she falls back onto the bed, pulling me down with her. I settle between her legs, wishing I could bury myself inside her, but I know I'll never have the chance. But I don't dwell on that fact, trailing my lips down her cheek to her jaw and then to her neck.

"Wait," she says, pushing against my chest.

Fuck. I knew she'd come to her senses, but I'd hoped I'd get a little further before she pulled back.

I lift up, giving her my eyes. "What's wrong?"

"I want the lights on."

Hell yes! Thank God she's comfortable in her skin. If we are going to do anything, I don't want the lights off. I want to revel in her beauty and watch her come apart because of the way I touch her.

I smile, looking at her beautiful face in the soft glow

of the moonlight. "I like the way you think," I tell her, pushing myself up.

She crawls back, reaching for the nightstand, and switches on the lamp. Her eyes are on me, roaming over my bare chest, drinking me in. "Better," she rasps.

I expect her to slide back down under me, but she doesn't. She reaches for the hem of her shirt, lifting it over her head, exposing the same black lace bra she wore to Inked, before she tosses her shirt to the floor next to the bed.

I kneel on the mattress, my eyes roaming her body the same way hers are moving across mine. "Come here," I tell her.

She crawls across the mattress, looking like a sexual goddess instead of the nerdy girl bookworm she portrays herself as.

Once in front of me, she rises to her knees, placing her hands on my shoulders. "Here?" she asks, her voice deep and needy as she leans forward, her lips near mine.

"Closer," I whisper.

She inches closer, our knees touching, eyes locked on each other. "Here?" she asks again, and my dick's already hard in anticipation of whatever is going to happen next.

I wrap one arm around her back, flattening my palm on her spine, and pull her forward. Her eyes drop to my mouth, waiting for the kiss she knows I'm going to give her. "Closer," I tell her again, lifting my hand to her chin, holding her gaze.

As I move my face forward, she tilts her head, waiting for my lips to touch hers. But just as I'm about to plant them on her, I bend my neck, trailing a line of kisses down her jaw.

She tips her head back, welcoming the caress of my lips against her skin. I move my mouth from her jaw to her neck, sucking and nipping the tender flesh below her jaw near her eye.

She shivers in my embrace, her body relaxing in my arms. Arlo's giving herself to me to explore with my mouth, and I take it unapologetically.

I lean her back, hovering over her, kissing her neck. I make my way to her collarbone. She arches her back, welcoming and wanting more. I smile against her skin and take my time with my exploration of her body.

Her arms fall to her sides as my lips glide lower, finding the edge of her lace bra. Instead of moving the cloth away, I nip at the material, capturing some of her skin. She moans when I make contact with her nipple. Her knees fall to the side, resting on the bed as she curls her fingers into the comforter.

"Don't stop," she breathes.

I moan with her nipple in my mouth, separated by the thin piece of lace. Using my teeth, I move the material to the side, exposing her naked flesh, and begin worshiping her body the only way I know how.

My hand drifts down her side, to the waistband of her pants. She lifts, giving me permission, and I take it, yanking her pants down far enough to have full access.

My fingers drift lower, caressing her through her matching black lace panties. She moans, pressing her clit against my hand, wanting more.

I lift up, staring down at her, waiting for her to tell me no as I hook my fingers into the sides of her underwear. But she says nothing as she stares up at me. I'm slow in pulling down her panties, exposing her most intimate parts to me. She blushes but doesn't cover her face. She isn't hiding or embarrassed by the way my eyes drift across her skin, soaking in every visible inch.

"You sure about this?"

"Yes," she whispers before I pull off her panties and pants, leaving her completely bare except for her bra.

I want this. Have wanted her since the moment she walked into my room at Inked, giving me those big green eyes and showing off her sexy bra.

Being here now, kissing her, touching her…it's surreal.

I slide my body down the bed, settling between her legs, my mouth ready to deliver the most delicious pleasure. She stares down the length of her body, her face soft but her eyes blazing with need and desire.

I move in, placing my lips on her pussy, taking my time not to devour her all at once. The moans fall easily from her lips as her hand finds my hair, holding me to her.

She's perfect like this.

Vulnerable and trusting.

Something neither of us is good at being, but somehow, with each other, it's different.

The significance of the moment and the connection isn't lost on me either.

Arlo is willing to give me pieces of herself she has rarely shared with anyone.

The specialness of it all hits me hard.

This is more than sex. This is the fusing of our connection.

Without much effort from me, she twists her fingers in my hair, pulling at my scalp as her body convulses, a moan falling from her lips.

Nothing in my life has ever tasted so sweet.

18

ALMOST A WEEK HAS GONE BY IN A COMPLETE BLUR. Every night after work, I've ended up on Arlo's doorstep, needing my fix after a long, grueling day.

Arlo always greets me in her dark-rimmed glasses, a messy bun, and the yoga pants I've grown so fond of in a very short time.

Her tattoo has healed nicely, no longer tender to the touch, giving me more of her skin to explore. We've moved slowly, and I am oddly okay with the pace, relishing her like a fine wine instead of chugging her in one sitting.

"What are you over there grinning about?" Lily asks, walking by me as I sit at my workstation, prepping for my next client.

"Nothing," I mutter, shaking my head and trying to

get the vision of Arlo in those damn pants out of my mind.

Lily stops in front of me, crossing her arms and peering down with a shit-eating grin. “You’re a shit liar, Mello. You were thinking about Arlo, weren’t you?”

I shrug, leaning back in my chair. “I can’t stop thinking about her, Lily. It’s your fault. You knew exactly what you were doing when you set us up, but I can’t be mad about it either.”

“I don’t know what you’re talking about,” she lies, her smile widening.

“You knew I’d fall for her.”

Lily shrugs one shoulder. “Maybe.”

“Slick fucker,” I mutter.

Jo lifts up her head from the appointment book, where she’s been filling in for Rebel this morning. “There’s a sucker born every day,” she says with a hint of laughter.

I sigh, rubbing the back of my neck. “I don’t even know what I’m doing with this chick. She’s way too good for me. She deserves someone…”

“Don’t you dare say it,” Lily hisses, glaring at me, with her finger aimed in my direction. “Don’t even think about walking away from her unless you have a really damn good reason. And, Mello, thinking she’s too good for you is not a damn good reason.”

“Oh.” I jerk my head back. “Are you the relationship police now?”

Gigi comes to stand behind Lily, narrowing her eyes at me. “What the hell did you just say?”

I scrub my hand down my face, knowing I’m about to catch the wrath of not one cousin, but multiple if I fuck this up. “For fuck’s sake,” I whisper against the palm of my hand.

“Arlo’s crazy about your dumb ass, and now you’re ready to break things off with her?” Gigi asks, hands on her hips, ready to do battle.

“That’s not what I said,” I snap. “I was over here, smiling and minding my own damn business, until Lily had to get all up in my shit.”

“Not smart, brother,” Pike mutters from my side. “Shit’s about to go down, and I’m not helping.”

“Pussy,” I shoot over my shoulder to Pike before returning my eyes to the two women in front of me, ignoring Jo as she shoots daggers my way from the front counter. “I’m not breaking Arlo’s heart. I don’t know how me having a fantasy about her—and enjoying it, mind you—turns into me ending things.”

“You said you thought she was too good for you,” Lily tells me like I wasn’t here for the entire conversation.

“She *is* too good for me, but you were too good for Jett, and look how that ended up,” I reply.

She lifts her hand, pointing to her wedding ring. “I’m happily married and regret nothing.”

"I know, Lily. I know. Can't I voice what I'm feeling to you without you two jumping in my shit?"

Lily and Gigi look at each other, passing some secret crazy-chick psychic-voodoo message back and forth before they turn back to me.

Gigi stalks over to me, climbing up on my table. "Listen, I need you to hear me when I say this."

"I'm listening," I growl.

"Eyes," she demands, being her usual bossy self.

I lift my eyes to her, trying to keep the snarl from my lips. "What?"

She shakes her head and takes a deep breath before she starts talking. "You deserve love."

"I am loved. I have all you fuckers so far up my ass, I can't help but feel the love all around me."

Gigi shakes her head. "No, dumbass. You deserve the love of a good woman. You've spent the last ten-plus years whoring yourself all around the county, burying your dick in anything that opened. It's time for that shit to stop. You are more than a fuckstick."

I blink, hating my cousins sometimes and their clever use of words. "I know I'm more than a fuckstick."

"Nothing about love makes sense, Mello. *Nothing.* It doesn't matter what either of you did before you met, but it sure as fuck matters what happens from that day forward. Are you treating her right?"

"Of course."

"Are you cheating on her?"

"No."

"Are you kind to her?"

"When am I not?"

"You've been known to be an asshole."

"Some women dig an asshole," I tell her. "And based on who you married, I'd say you're one of them."

"What the fuck did I ever do to you?" Pike asks, glaring at me as he wipes off his table, sterilizing it for his next client. "I'm minding my own damn business, and you have to drag me into shit?"

"You opened your mouth, brother," I repeat the same name he called me earlier when he entered into the conversation. "You became fair game."

"Pike is never an asshole to me," Gigi states, kicking her legs back and forth as she sits on my table, barely missing my knees with every swing. "If he were an asshole, he'd be gone in a flash."

Pike laughs. "Darlin', you like my dick too much to get rid of me."

She turns, deadpanning, "Ain't no dick worth staying with a miserable son of a bitch, darlin', not even yours."

His head jerks back, and he lifts his hands. "Noted."

"As I was saying, you're worthy of love…even Arlo's love. Don't you dare make a decision for her based on what you think she wants, needs, or deserves."

"Got it," I tell her, over the conversation. "But I was

actually thinking good shit about her…about us. So, really, this conversation is useless."

"You get something in your head and you're liable to run with it and not look back. I want to make sure you're running toward something and not away from possibly the best damn thing in your life."

"I'm not running anywhere, Gigi. It's been a week, and we're still feeling each other out."

"You steal her virginity yet?" Gigi asks me point-blank.

"No," I grunt. "And when and if she gives it, I won't be stealing it either."

"Don't you dare—" Gigi pokes me in the shoulder "—take it from her unless you're in this for the long haul. Don't be *that* guy."

I raise my hands again. "I never planned on it."

Lily exhales, clutching her chest. "I can't believe you haven't tried to have sex with her yet."

"I can't believe we're having this conversation in the middle of our business during business hours."

Lily swipes her hand in the air. "No one is here but us, and what's said between these walls stays between these walls."

"So, you're not going to tell Tamara, then?" I raise an eyebrow. "Because the last time I checked, she isn't within these walls."

She glances upward and squeezes her eyes shut. "She's the exception," she whispers.

"Figures," I mumble.

Rebel walks in and glances around, coming to a dead stop. "What happened? Who died?"

"No one," Lily tells her. "Just talking about Arlo and Mello."

"Did you fuck it up already?" Rebel asks me.

I cover my face with my hands and let my head fall forward. "Why do I work here again?"

"Because you love us," Rebel says.

Rocco's a few seconds behind her. "What's wrong?"

"Jesus Christ," I groan. "Why does there always have to be something wrong?"

"You fuck it up already?" Those words from his mouth are pointed at me.

"No. Fuck," I hiss, pushing off my chair and heading toward the back door, needing some fresh air.

As soon as my boots touch the cement, I tip my head back, feeling the warmth of the sunshine on my face. I stand perfectly still, enjoying the peacefulness after the clusterfuck inside, but it doesn't last long before the door swings open behind me.

"Don't listen to them," Rocco says, walking to my side. "They're nosy."

"Yeah." I let out a bitter laugh. "That's one word for them."

He nudges me in the ribs with his bony elbow. "Everything okay with you?"

"I'm fine. Everything's great." I look over at him,

finding him standing the same way I had been, with his face upward, soaking in the sun.

He opens one eye, turning his head slightly to look at me. "You sure?"

"Yeah, Roc."

"And things with Arlo?"

I kick at the few random stones near my boots, smiling. "Better than I could've imagined."

He punches my arm. "You don't know how fucking happy I am to hear that. I know you're probably scared shitless right now, but you need to let yourself be happy and find peace in joy."

I scrunch my nose, staring at him. "Have you been watching those inspirational videos online again?"

He shakes his head and laughs. "Nah, man. Just got the love of a good woman and realized everything I missed all those years. You're in that weird in-between place right now. Just lean into it."

"If I lean any further, I'll fall over."

He swings his arm around my shoulder. "The joys of love."

"Whoa. Whoa. Whoa." I pull away, letting his arm drop. "I'm not in love. It's been a week, bro. I'm not running, but I'm sure as hell not rushing things either."

"I know what love looks like, and it's written all over your face. I'll give you time to come to the realization of how you really feel, but just remember, Arlo may not have the patience to wait forever for you to say the words."

I run my fingers through my hair and exhale. "A week, man. A week. No one falls in love in a week."

"Right now, you're infatuated. Things are new. Shit's exciting. But when the dust settles and you have a choice of life with her or without, that's when you'll know how you really feel."

"How did you know you loved Rebel?" I ask him.

"If I'm being totally honest with myself, I think I've loved her since the first time I met her. Leaving her at the hospital after the accident, man…that shit killed me."

"But you never even talked to her after that. If you loved her, why would you not at least reach out to her once in those ten long years?"

He shrugs. "Figured she was better off without me."

"You were wrong."

"I know that now, but I regret nothing."

"You don't?"

"Nope. If I'd chased her, she wouldn't have Adaline, and maybe whatever spark we had would've fizzled out and died a long time ago. Neither of us was ready to move on and accept the happiness we both deserved."

"Makes sense in your own fucked-up way."

"Never claimed to make sense or be that smart, but I know how to love, and so do you. Mom and Dad taught us everything we need to know, but if you fuck up, know Mom's going to beat your ass first, and then I will."

"It's a common theme among everyone when it comes to Arlo and me."

Rocco laughs again. "Well, you're a jackass, but I know you'll do the right thing instead of running away like a pansy."

"Have I ever run from anything?"

"Relationships," he teases, but he's telling the truth. "And intimacy."

That shit was my kryptonite, and I had run as fast as I could in the opposite direction. I honestly never even let a person outside my family get close enough to me to have to worry about intimacy or relationships becoming a problem.

Rocco places his hand on my shoulder. "I can tell you're different when it comes to Arlo. It's nice to see."

"How am I different?"

He smiles, rubbing his chin. "Carmello, there's no one else in the world I know better than you, and vice versa. You light up when you talk about her, and you're a little fucked in the head too. You get all macho crazy, which isn't something you've ever really done, not even for the best piece of ass."

"I'm fucked, aren't I?"

He nods. "Totally, but it's okay. Like I said…lean in."

"Guys," Rebel says, poking her head out of the back door, looking between Rocco and me. "Your appointments are here."

"We're coming, babe," Rocco tells her, giving me a wink, still madly in love with his wife.

She nods and goes back inside, leaving us alone.

"I'm happy things worked out with the two of you."

"I didn't realize how unhappy I was until Rebel walked back into my life, along with Adaline."

"You have a good woman. She has to be to put up with your ass."

He stares at me, not looking amused at all. "You're not easy either. If Arlo can deal with your insane bullshit and bad attitude, then you better do whatever you can to keep her around. I don't know many women who would put up with your nonsense."

"They only knew the pieces of me I wanted them to know," I tell him.

"So, just your dick, then?"

I nod. "Basically."

He punches my arm as he starts toward the back door of the shop. "You're an asshole."

"Love you too," I call out, letting him go inside first and giving myself a last moment alone.

Life does taste a little sweeter with Arlo at my side, something I never imagined with someone who was only supposed to be my fake girlfriend.

But I know my cousin Lily, and she had been calculated in her pick, knowing I'd fall for Arlo. I can't even be mad about it either, because for the first time in a very long time…I'm happy.

19

ARLO CURLS INTO MY SIDE, SLINGING HER ARM ACROSS my middle. "You okay?" she whispers against my skin.

"I'm good. You?" I'm staring up at the ceiling, trying to picture the future with Arlo.

And I see it too. Marriage. Kids. Growing old together. All the happy things my cousins and brother have been doing but I thought were never for me.

Arlo hits different from anyone else, giving me a vision of the future, and it is one I like.

"My day was good, but it's better now that you're here," she says softly.

I tip my head down and brush my lips against her forehead. "Ditto, sugar."

She drags her fingernails across my skin, tracing the ridges of my ribs. "I thought about what you said the other day."

I focus again on the ceiling fan above us, trying to remember what I said to Arlo that has her still thinking about those words days later.

"And what was that?"

She peers up at me, not lifting her head from my shoulder. "You said your dad could maybe help me find my parents."

"He could." My fingers glide across the skin of her back, following the path of her spine. "If that's what you want, he'll make it happen."

"I don't know if I want to, but I can't stop thinking about them."

"Whatever you want, Arlo. We can talk to my dad at dinner tomorrow. Just be sure it's what you want."

"Do you think it's stupid?"

"Why would I think it's stupid?"

She pushes up on her elbow, staring down at me. "If they really wanted to find me, they would've by now. You know? I'm just setting myself up for failure and rejection."

I raise my hand and cradle her face. "No one could turn you away. You're too sweet and beautiful."

She gives me a sorrowful smile, her green eyes searching mine. "They probably forgot about me by now."

"You're unforgettable," I whisper. "And I don't think any parent, even someone who gives up a child for adoption, could forget their own baby."

Her smile changes, and the sadness vanishes from her face. "You constantly surprise me."

"How's that?" I ask, running my thumb across her cheekbone.

"I really thought you'd be a jerk once I got to know you."

I am a jerk. I won't say those words out loud, but I am. I accept the man I've become, built on the sadness of losing Carrie and the guilt I feel over her death. It is like my ability to love is buried with her, sealed away and never to be seen again.

But no matter what, I haven't been able to show that side of myself to Arlo. It feels wrong and dirty. You can't shovel shit at someone so sweet, especially when they don't do anything to deserve it.

I don't have an endgame with Arlo besides spending time with her and hoping I learn something about myself before our agreement becomes something more…something real.

With the other women, I always had something I wanted. Just pussy and nothing more. A fuck or a suck, and off they went, away from me. Exactly how I wanted it and at the speed I chose.

"If you thought I was a jerk, why would you say yes to Lily's scheme?"

"Scheme?" Arlo laughs softly, placing her hand on my chest. "There was no scheme. She thought you were redeemable, and like me, she believes our pasts don't define our futures. She just felt like you needed a few tweaks. And you were so good to me, I wanted to see if you were the man I thought you were."

I lunge forward, pushing Arlo onto her back and put my body weight on her. I settle between her thighs, our bodies separated by a few scraps of cloth. "And what tweaks do I need?"

She looks up at me, her feet hooked behind my back, a smirk on her lips. "A few," she teases, running her fingernails up and down my lower back.

My mouth finds her neck, and I kiss the spot right below her ear that makes her moan. "And what would they be?" I murmur against her skin.

"You could kiss lower," she whispers, her body squirming underneath mine.

There isn't an inch of her body I don't want to kiss. My mouth needs to be intimately acquainted with every patch of her skin, knowing how it tastes or feels against my lips. But we haven't gotten there yet. I've learned restraint, something I'd thought impossible.

I move my hands to her arms, stretching them above her head, and I hold them there as my mouth drifts lower. She arches her back, pushing her breasts upward, offering them to me for worship.

"Like this?" I sweep my bottom lip over the swell of her breasts, loving the way she feels and hating myself for liking this so much.

She grinds her middle against me, making it impossible to hold in my moan or stop my dick from getting rock hard. "Lower," she tells me.

She's beautiful like this. Natural and uninhibited, a wildness she never shows to the outside world but saves for me. There's something precious about this side of her that she only shares with me. A sacredness to the way she stares into my eyes, burning for my touch.

I take her nipple between my lips and run my tongue across the top, wanting nothing more than to strip her bare and bury myself deep inside her.

She moans, her back arching like it has every other time I've had my mouth on her. Responsive isn't even a strong enough word to describe Arlo when I taste her body.

There's pounding at the front door, and Arlo stiffens underneath me. "Are you expecting company?"

I lift up, hanging my head, and I release Arlo's arms. "No, but it's never a good sign at this hour."

"You better go," she says, pushing against my shoulders when the pounding starts again.

I growl under my breath, hating whoever's at my door after midnight. "I'll be right back," I tell her, adjusting my dick as soon as my feet are on the floor.

She sits up, reaching for the sheet to cover her breasts. "I'm not going anywhere," she whispers.

I stalk out of the bedroom, down the hallway, and open the door without looking.

Standing on my front porch are two of my cousins, one leaning on the other, barely able to stay upright.

"Hey, cousin," Rosie says with a big, fake-ass smile. "Luna got into a bit of trouble tonight."

Shocking…not.

"And?" I ask, getting smacked right in the face with the stench of liquor coming off Luna, wrinkling my nose.

Rosie looks up at me from under her eyelashes, unable to make full eye contact. "I'm wondering if we can crash here tonight?"

I step forward, leaning against the doorframe as Luna sways, and somehow, Rosie keeps her from falling over. "And why would I let you do that? Why didn't you go to your sister's?"

"Fuck that," Luna slurs, her eyes not focusing when she looks at me. "I don't need the lecture from Gigi."

"Shut it," I tell Luna. "You don't get a vote."

"Fucker," she mutters under her breath.

Rosie raises her eyebrows. "If you can't tell, Luna's pissed at Gigi. And I can't take her home like this, or Mom and Dad will lose their shit. Please, please, please, can we stay here tonight?" Rosie begs.

"I have company."

Rosie blinks, finally looking at me. "And that's new how?"

I stare at her, my face conveying my unhappiness.

Rosie swallows and sighs. “You won’t even know we’re here,” she promises.

“We’ll be quiet,” Luna adds. “I just need to lie down before I…” She covers her mouth as her cheeks bulge.

“For fuck’s sake,” I hiss, stepping forward and scooping Luna into my arms before she barfs all over my hardwood floors. “This shit has got to stop.”

“It wasn’t her fault this time,” Rosie says, following me into the house as I carry Luna through the living room. “I swear. This time is not like the other times.”

The two of them have been nothing but trouble since the day they hit puberty. But instead of the rest of the family knowing about their party-girl, wild-child ways, they’ve used me and the other older cousins as cover.

“If your father finds out, he’s going to beat all of our asses, and I’m not looking to be black-and-blue.”

“He won’t.” Those words come from Rosie, and I know she won’t be the one spilling her guts because she’d be in just as much trouble as me, minus the bruises.

They are daddy’s girls like Gigi. Always the apples of their father’s eye as they did crazy shit on the down-low, keeping their status as good kids instead of hell-raisers.

They are nothing like their mom. Aunt Suzy is sweet, kind, and she has an innocence to her no one else with my family’s genetics has. But these girls don’t care, nor did they get virtue from their mom.

"Bathroom," Luna groans, limp as a rag doll in my arms.

Arlo steps into the hallway, adjusting a T-shirt she must've grabbed from my room. "Everything okay?" she asks, eyeing Luna in my arms.

"She's drunk," I tell Arlo, motioning to the right with my head, needing to get around her with the dead weight.

She steps aside, letting me stalk past her to get the girl who hasn't learned her limits to the toilet before she expels the contents of her stomach in the hallway. "What can I do?" Arlo asks Rosie.

"Nothing. She'll be fine. This happens sometimes."

Sometimes? I'd laugh if I weren't so pissed at the two of them.

"It does?" Arlo asks her, clueless. "How often?"

"This time wasn't her fault, though," Rosie explains, but she doesn't answer Arlo's question.

The two of them have become masters of deflection. If they had been born with dicks…

They would be me.

The reality of that truth hits me square in the chest like a punch, knocking the wind out of me for a moment.

I push open the bathroom door with my foot and use my elbow to turn on the light before depositing Luna on the small rug in front of the toilet.

She groans, immediately moving her upper body

over the toilet seat, hugging it like it's her lifeline. "Go," she tells me as her back starts to heave.

I don't have to be told twice. I leave her there, clinging to the toilet to do her business for however long it takes her to get rid of the poison in her system this time.

"I should go help her," Rosie says, lifting her chin toward the bathroom as I step back into the hallway.

I grab Rosie's arm before she walks around me. "When she's done, I expect answers before anyone goes to sleep tonight." I glare at her, letting the little spitfire know I'm pissed, in case she hadn't clued into that little fact already.

Rosie nods with a heavy swallow, staring up at me with a deep frown. "Okay," she whispers.

She's gone as soon as I let her loose, closing the bathroom door behind her.

"I take it this isn't the first time they've shown up at your place like this?" Arlo asks before walking toward me.

I shake my head. "Those two are nothing but trouble, Ar. Total shitshow."

She wraps her arms around my middle, resting her cheek against my chest. "They seemed really sweet at your grandma's."

"They're good at appearing one way in front of the family and another way with those who know them best.

If you looked up party animals in the dictionary, you'd find a picture of those two."

"There are no pictures in the dictionary, honey," Arlo teases, squeezing me tightly as her body shakes with laughter.

"Arlo," I warn, hanging on by a thread because those two interrupted what I'd hoped would be a very eventful night. "Come on. Let's go to the living room unless you want to listen to the show. There's going to be lots of groveling and promises about sobriety she'll never follow through on."

"Poor thing," Arlo whispers, peeling her body away from mine. "Is she even old enough to be drinking?"

"Not until next month." I take her hand, leading her toward the couch, and collapse backward, bringing her with me. "I imagine you were never like them."

Arlo settles in my lap, her legs on the cushions, pressing against my thighs. "There was a time when I was a little out of control."

I raise my eyebrows. "You?"

She nods, smirking. "Me."

My hands find her ass, cupping her cheeks in my palms. "Tell me about *that* Arlo."

She shakes her head. "She wasn't very nice."

"Impossible," I whisper, staring into her haunting green eyes.

Arlo has been nothing but reserved and sweet. Thinking about a side of her that is anything but is truly impossible for me to imagine. Visualizing her in the foster care system is also something my brain can't quite grasp. I would've bet a chunk of money that she came from a family much like my own, and I would've lost and lost big.

She leans forward, resting her forehead against mine. "I went through a rebellious phase when I was seventeen, realizing I was about to lose the little bit I had. I started hanging around with the wrong crowd and…" She pauses and pulls her head back, looking me straight in the eyes before continuing. "I didn't put much thought into how my behavior would only make it easier for the family I was living with to let me go."

I tighten my grip on her ass, bringing her closer as my chest aches for what she went through. "Sucks, sugar."

"Yeah," she whispers, her gaze dipping to my chest before coming back to my face. "Didn't realize what I'd done until it was too late. Kids do stupid shit sometimes, Mello." She ticks her head toward the hallway where Luna and Rosie are. "Even good kids like your cousins."

"They're not kids anymore, Arlo. At some point, they have to grow up."

"Rosie is sober."

I nod slowly. "She's slightly more responsible than her sister, but they've both been pulling shit for years."

Way too many years for my liking. If Uncle Joe and Aunt Suzy had any clue, these two would've been grounded most of their high school years. But now, they're older, wilder, and usually no more smarter in their decision-making process.

"Well—" Arlo places her palms flat on my pecs, totally feeling me up, but pretending she isn't "—maybe you need to step into their life and set them straight or tell their parents about who their daughters really are."

I turn my head to the side, sucking in air between my teeth. "Can't snitch, babe. My family does not snitch on one another, especially not the cousins."

She slides forward right over my dick that's aching for some relief but knows we're getting none. "Then you're going to have to be the one to show them the way, or at least tell Gigi, so she can handle them and put them on the right path."

"Fuck," I hiss, hating the idea of getting involved in their bullshit.

I have always been good with women, but my cousins are another breed. I am stepping out of my comfort zone, never having had to deal with sisters. That is the good thing about only having Trace. He is an asshole, but I know how he thinks since he has a dick too.

The bathroom door opens, and Arlo gives me a look. The same look my mother gives me when she's telling me to do something without actually saying the words.

A second later, Arlo's weight shifts, and the warmth

of her body is gone as she moves to the cushion next to me.

"Out here," I call out before they have a chance to disappear into one of my guest rooms like they have in the past.

"But Luna should…"

"Out here," I growl, not even bothering to turn around to look at them. "We need to talk."

"Fucking great," Luna groans. "Just what I fuckin' need."

I bite my lip, tilting my head, feeling the tension rise in my shoulders. Arlo touches my hand with hers, giving my fingers a light squeeze.

"Calm," she whispers.

Calm? I have always been calm, and that's why I am still dealing with their shit nearly five years later.

This must be a sliver of what it feels like to have kids and deal with their nonsense on a daily basis. Am I built for this type of responsibility, disappointment, and heartache? I'm not sure the answer is yes.

Luna's still leaning on Rosie as they walk slowly into the living room, their eyes moving from Arlo to me and back to Arlo.

"Sit," I bite out, done with their shit.

"What?" Luna snaps before her ass even touches the couch cushion directly across from me. "I'm tired and need to sleep."

"Fuck that," I hiss.

"God, you're such a downer. Find yourself an innocent snatch, and you turn into a killjoy."

What the fuck?

My body rises on its own, her words fueling a fire deep inside me, but before I have a chance to lunge over the coffee table, Arlo yanks me back down.

"Carmello," she whispers, holding on to me tightly.

I take a deep breath, running my other hand down my sweatpants so I don't reach over the coffee table and—

Fuck, what the hell do you do when you have girls?

As a boy, growing up Caldo, if we talked shit, my dad would call us out. And if we continued, that's when things went south in a hurry.

He didn't hesitate to let us know he could beat us to a pulp if he wanted, but he never did.

The fear was there and felt very real, but not once did he lay his hands on us.

We knew enough to put our attitudes away and beg for forgiveness. This clearly isn't a skill my two little cousins have learned.

"Talk, and make it good," I tell them, relaxing back into the couch with Arlo at my side and our hands locked together.

"Well, Luna met this biker," Rosie says, and I squeeze my eyes shut, praying for patience.

20

"Oh dear," Arlo whispers, covering her mouth with one hand and leaning forward, totally invested in the story Rosie's still telling a half hour later.

"You going to keep dancing around the truth?" I ask her as I open my eyes and narrow them on her and her drunk-ass sister.

Rosie's eyes widen. "I'm telling you the truth," she sasses, when she has no room to sass.

Fucking girls, man.

They're the worst.

Guys get a bad rap, but we're at least up front about our shitty behavior. Not girls, though.

I cock my head and cross my arms over my chest, trying to remain calm, but I'm close to snapping. "You're taking the long road to get to the final destination."

"Just tell him so I can sleep," Luna begs, leaning over and staring at her legs. "He's going to find out anyway."

I turn my head the other way, cocking it to the right side. "And how will I find out?"

Luna shrugs. "Small-town bullshit," she mutters and lifts her head, looking like absolute shit.

My cousins are beautiful, but right now, they look like they partied too hard, which they did. The path they are going down is bad, and somehow, I've been tasked with getting their shit together when mine isn't even tight.

Fucking ridiculous.

"Maybe you should wait until you're back on campus to act like idiots. Then you wouldn't be on my couch, asking for me to give you shelter and lie for your asses."

Rosie rolls her eyes. "We don't ask for much."

My entire body tenses. I take a deep breath, reminding myself these aren't my kids. "How many times have I shown up at your door after midnight asking the same?"

Rosie chews on her lip but doesn't take her eyes off me. "You're right. We're selfish assholes."

"Damn fucking straight, I'm right."

Arlo puts her hand on my knee, but she doesn't look back at me, keeping her body facing my cousins.

It's a silent gesture to remind me to keep that damn

calm I've never been good at keeping and probably never will be.

"Go on," Arlo tells Rosie. "We're not here to judge you."

I twist my lips, keeping them shut. Rosie's gaze moves from Arlo to me, and she's expecting me to say something, but I don't.

"Fine," she breathes and rubs at her eyes with her palms. "We went to a party down by the caves."

I grunt, knowing the spot all too well.

Rosie's eyes are on me again, but I stay silent, letting her talk. "We brought a six-pack to split, promising we wouldn't drink any more than that. This is the last place we wanted to end up tonight."

"Then what happened?" Arlo asks before I can say something completely sarcastic.

"We had two beers each, and Luna had been flirting with this guy."

"He was hot," Luna adds, swaying next to her sister with a lopsided grin.

"Luna, shut it," Rosie tells her, pushing her with her shoulder, making her lean to the other side of the couch before she goes on. "Anyway, I walked off for a few minutes to talk to some old friends, leaving Luna with the hot biker guy."

"Dumb," I mutter under my breath.

Rosie shakes her head. "When I came back, she told me she was having some punch, but she was acting funny. She offered me her cup and I coated my lips without taking a sip, and I knew. I fucking knew she was going to be wasted."

"Well, you were right. She's wasted."

"I know," Rosie says, but at least there's remorse in her voice this time.

"I tried to dump it out, but Luna flipped out, taking the cup from my hands and downing the entire thing in one giant gulp."

"It was fruit punch. What's the big deal?" Luna asks, not even able to keep her eyes open anymore.

I hope like hell she'll pay for her behavior tomorrow. She isn't blameless. If Rosie could smell the alcohol, so could Luna, but she didn't care. She deserves a wicked hangover and to be around our loud-ass family while dealing with it, too.

"It had a splash of fruit punch," Rosie tells her.

Luna shrugs. "Whatever," she mumbles. "It tasted good."

"Don't listen to her. She's not thinking right." Rosie excuses her sister's behavior, something she's done a lot of in her life.

I understand them, though. They are twins like Rocco and me. We always have each other's back… always. I don't care what he does wrong; I will never turn on him and will do whatever I can to shield him from bad, just like he's done for me. That's how the twin life is and always will be.

"I'm not entirely convinced they didn't slip something else into the drink either. She was way too shit-faced for the amount of time I was gone. It couldn't have been more than twenty minutes, and Luna has a higher tolerance than that."

"They may have drugged her," Arlo agrees, her hand tightening on my knee, sensing my mood change.

"Fuck," I hiss, my anger shifting from the two dumbasses in front of me to whoever slipped something into my cousin's drink.

"Don't do anything," Rosie tells me. "They're not worth the hassle."

I lean forward and grind my teeth together as I stare at my cute little cousin who wants to grow up way too fast. "You don't fuck with a Gallo and get away with that shit, Rosie. You can fuck with the men, but fuck with one of our women, and there are going to be issues."

"No," she snaps. "That's not fair. Luna fucked up. She knows better than to take a drink from a stranger. And I didn't recognize the guy. I'd never seen him before, and finding him probably won't be easy."

"Small town, Rosie. If he was there, someone invited him, and I'll have no problem tracking him."

Arlo's face pales as she turns to look at me. "Carmello," she whispers, begging me not to do what I want to do.

"Arlo, it's a family matter and a decision I won't and

can't make alone."

"I don't want to visit you in jail or the morgue," she says, her eyes filled with fear.

"Sugar," I say, lifting her hand to my lips. "I promise that won't happen."

"Can I go to sleep now?" Luna asks, slumped over on the cushion next to her, hardly even awake now.

"No," I tell Luna, turning back toward Rosie, who's barely moving. "Keep talking."

"You can be mad at Luna for being stupid, but being this messed up isn't her fault, Mello. We made a pact to keep our noses clean this summer, saving the hard stuff for campus. I swear to God, this wasn't supposed to happen. You believe me, don't you?"

I stare at my cousin, having known her since the day she took her first breath. She's never lied to me, always coming clean when she fucks up, and I can read her tells after twenty years. "I believe you."

"Phew," she wheezes, her shoulders slumping forward. "God, you're worse than Dad."

"Rosie, you have your dad wrapped around your finger. If he knew…"

"He can never," she whispers. "Promise me."

"A façade only lasts so long before it crumbles."

Arlo yawns and covers her mouth. "Maybe we should get some sleep and finish this talk in the morning when we're all coherent."

Rosie stares at me, pleading with me with her eyes.

“Yeah. Fine. I’m exhausted. Tomorrow, we’ll talk to Luna when she’s more with it, and then we’ll go to Grandma’s. But—” I point a finger at Rosie “—you call or text your parents where you are so they’re not worried.”

“Already done,” she says, glancing down.

Arlo reaches over and grabs my hand before standing. “Come on, honey. We could all use some rest.”

I’m on my feet, letting her guide me away from the couch, but I stop before I get too far. “Need help getting her to bed?”

“No.” Rosie stands, pushing Luna over and lifting her legs onto the couch. “She can sleep here tonight. I’m not sharing a bed with her. She’s a kicker, and I don’t want to be all bruised tomorrow.”

Arlo chuckles behind me, and I shake my head at my cousin. “You know where everything is. Talk tomorrow. Night, kid.”

“Night, Mello. Thank you and I love you.”

“Love you too, Rosie.”

She exhales, looking more relaxed, and for a moment, I feel bad about being so harsh on her, but then I remember the numerous times this has happened before.

“Night, Arlo,” Rosie says softly, walking behind us down the hallway to the bedrooms.

“Night, babe,” Arlo returns before yanking me into the bedroom.

She closes the door and leaps into my arms, wrapping her legs around me. Her hands are on my face, holding my cheeks. "I'm so proud of you."

"For what?" I laugh, looking at my girl like she's fucking nutty.

"You sounded so adult out there. You stayed pretty level-headed and handled them well."

"If you hadn't been here…" My words die when her lips collide with mine, the force with which she takes my mouth pushing me backward.

I fall onto the bed, landing on my back with her on top of me, luckily moving her legs as we go down so I don't crush them under my weight.

"You'd be an awesome dad," she whispers against my lips.

"I don't want girls," I tell her, sliding my hands underneath the T-shirt she put on earlier. "Never girls."

"Don't say that. Girls can be great too."

"When?"

She laughs, and it's a beautiful sound. "When they're little."

"Yeah, then they grow up and turn into them."

"So, you mean a female version of you, but prettier."

"Exactly," I groan.

Her lips come down softly on mine, nipping at my bottom lip. "It's a shame our evening was interrupted."

My fingers sweep under her breast. "We can pick up

right where we left off."

"No," she says, climbing off me, leaving me with wood. "Not with the girls here."

"I'm back to being pissed at them."

Arlo laughs again, curling back into my side. "There's always tomorrow, honey," she whispers as I reach up, turning off the lamp on my nightstand.

"Tell my dick that, sugar."

She sits up, bringing her mouth right above my cock. "Tomorrow, little guy."

Little guy?

I know she hasn't seen my dick up close and personal in the bare flesh, but nothing about it is little. The outline is clear as day in my gray sweatpants, and the woman has practically ridden on me, dry humping me just a few nights ago.

"Whoa. Whoa. Whoa," I warn her. "Never, don't ever, call him 'little guy.' Instant boner killer."

She peers up my body, a wicked grin on her face. "Then my business here is done."

I place my hands at her sides, pulling her back against me. "Women are cruel creatures."

"We can be," she says, smiling against the skin of my chest, dragging those fingernails across my abdomen. "But sometimes the torture can be delicious."

"I'll remember you said that next time we're alone."

She tips her head back, biting her lip. "I look forward to it, honey."

"Go to sleep, Arlo."

She shifts, coming in for another kiss, and I give her my mouth one last time.

"Night, honey."

"Night, sugar."

But I don't fall asleep. I lie there for what feels like hours, thinking about my dick, Arlo, and whose ass I need to beat for getting Luna all fucked up.

The night is long, but I worry tomorrow will be longer.

"I NEED IBUPROFEN," Luna says, walking into the kitchen after peeling her body off the couch. Her eyes are barely open, the sunshine clearly too much for her hungover ass to handle.

"You know where it is," I reply, standing next to Arlo and prepping the toast for breakfast as she scrambles the eggs.

"Oh God," Luna whines. "Eggs are not a smell I want right now."

"You're going to eat something and get your ass right before we go to Grandma's."

"I need to go home and change."

"Not looking like that," I tell her.

"He's right," Rosie adds, sitting at the kitchen table, having watched and talked to us for the last thirty minutes while she sipped her coffee. "If Mom or Dad sees you right now…"

"Fuck," Luna hisses and grabs her head. "What the hell did I have last night?"

"A hot biker." Rosie throws out there.

Luna's hands drop to her sides, and her eyes widen. "Did I—"

"No. You didn't sleep with him, but do you remember the fruit punch he gave you?"

Luna blinks, staring across the room at her sister, still in a haze. "Kinda."

"Well, I think it was spiked with more than booze."

"Shit," Luna snaps and crumples forward, resting her elbows on the countertop below the cabinet where I store the ibuprofen. "No wonder I feel like death."

"Ibuprofen, food, and a hot shower should help you feel slightly better, but it's going to be a rough day, Lun. You better lie low at Gram's and stay outside where it's quieter."

"I can't be inside with everyone."

"Don't stick around anyone too long because the booze is still coming out of your pores," I tell her, wrinkling my nose.

"Fuck off," she teases, lifting the middle finger closest to me in the air. "What a freaking suck."

"Eggs are almost ready," Arlo announces. "Toast done?"

"Done, and bacon is on the table," I reply. "Rosie,

grab some plates and silverware."

"On it," Rosie says, rising from her chair and grabbing everything we need.

Luna reaches into the cabinet for the pills, resting her body on the edge of the counter for balance. "You're all moving too fast."

"The world is moving too fast for you today, babe. Have some bacon and toast if you can't stomach the eggs. The protein and carbs will be good for you."

"I need coffee to wash down these pills," she states.

Arlo looks over at her, moving the eggs around the pan. "You should use water."

All three of us stare at her in silence.

"What?" she asks, looking at each of us. "That's what the bottle says."

"Ar, no one follows the directions. Liquid is liquid," Rosie informs her.

"I follow the directions," Arlo replies.

"Shocking," Rosie teases on a whisper as she heads back to the table with plates, forks, and napkins. "So does my mom, but no one else."

"Do you take them with water?" Arlo asks me.

I shake my head. "I grab whatever is closest."

Arlo gawks at me. "For real?"

"Yeah, babe. I'm a dude, too. We're not going to stop for some water. We're going to grab whatever and choke those pills down."

She blinks, her mouth hanging open.

"Arlo, you're way too grown up for Carmello," Rosie tells her, setting the table. "He may look old, but he's not fully grown."

"I don't *look* old," I correct her. "I'm not fucking old."

Rosie laughs. "Cousin, you're in your thirties."

"I'm thirty-one, not in them."

"You are, but not deep. Still makes you middle-aged."

It's my turn to blink, jerking my head back. "What the hell, kid? I give you a place to stay and breakfast, and you have to throw shade my way?"

"Oh, stop. Thirty isn't old. I think the guy Luna was flirting with last night was older than you."

"Oh boy," Arlo whispers.

I turn my gaze to Luna, and my eyes immediately narrow. "What. The. Fuck?"

Luna shrugs before jamming two pills into her mouth and washing them down with coffee. She mumbles, the words not audible behind the mug.

I point the butter knife at Rosie and then Luna. "Thirty is way too old for either of you. Stick to your own age group."

"Have you been around twenty-year-old men lately?" Rosie asks as she slides back into her chair.

"Just the ones who come into the shop and the others in our family. Besides them, no," I tell her honestly.

"They suck. Like not a little suck, but suck hard. All they care about is gaming, and they're broke as fuck. I ain't about to sit on the couch all night, playing video games or watching them play video games. And besides that, I want a man who's going to treat me like a queen, and so does Luna."

"I'm sure you could've found your Prince Charming at the caves last night, right?"

Rosie rolls her eyes at me. "You're being an asshole again."

I touch my chest, pretending to be hurt. "Babe, all guys are assholes. If you think otherwise, you're mistaken. Who in our family who has a dick isn't an asshole?"

She taps her lip, glaring at me as I carry the toast to the table. "No one," she mutters. "But I'm not giving up on mankind just yet."

"You're in for a big letdown."

"Then why do people get married?"

"Because they find the one asshole they can put up with on a daily basis. You just have to find the right asshole for you, with the knowledge that he, too, is an asshole, no matter how sweet he seems at the beginning."

"Arlo, do you know Carmello's an asshole?"

Arlo chuckles as she slides the scrambled eggs into a bowl. "I know he is, but he's super sweet too. I don't see his asshole side too often."

“I’m good at hiding it,” I whisper to Rosie, giving her a wink. “Suck her in with the sweet first.”

“God, I hate men,” Luna says, coming to sit next to her sister. “You guys really are all assholes who only think with your dicks.”

“Basically,” I tell her. “The sooner you accept that as fact, the better off you’ll be. Always be leery of the nice ones. They’re wolves in sheep’s clothing.”

“Does that include you?” Luna asks me.

“That has been me, but not with Arlo.”

“Why not with Arlo?” she shoots back.

“I don’t know, kid.”

“You’re sweet and patient too,” Arlo adds as she sets the bowl of eggs in the middle of the table. Her arms then come around my shoulders, her cheek pressed to mine. “I wasn’t prepared for you.”

I turn my face slightly so our lips are almost touching. “Hooked you already, didn’t I?”

“You did,” she whispers.

“You two are gross,” Luna says.

Arlo’s smile touches her eyes as she looks at me. “I like being gross with you.”

I plant a big sloppy kiss on her, hearing the two girls gag and not giving a fuck. This is my house, and if they don’t like seeing the mushy shit, they shouldn’t get drunk and need a place to hide out from their parents.

“Eat,” I tell them. “And then showers. We have to be at Gram’s in a few hours.”

21

"Where are we going?" Arlo asks, wrapping her arms around my waist as I fire up the bike.

"Somewhere special."

"But I thought we'd hang out with everyone," she says in my ear, making herself heard over the roar of the engine.

I turn my head, looking at her over my shoulder. "I don't want to share you all day, sugar."

She smiles, her green eyes lighting up. "Okay."

"Okay," I say back to her, giving her a wink. "Hold on, babe."

She tightens her arms around my middle and places her cheek on my back. I love this. The way she feels against my body, plastered to me like a second skin.

I move slower, weaving in and out of traffic less

than I would if I were alone. I have precious cargo on the back, something I don't ever want to injure.

There are still times, a decade later, when Carrie's death creeps up on me and the guilt of not controlling the car crashes down, having the ability to suck me in. The times are fewer. The episodes shorter. But they still come and go.

I've never much cared about my own personal safety, but I worry about my friends, family, and now Arlo.

I take no extra chances, checking my surroundings more than usual and driving defensively instead of offensively. Is this what happens when you love someone? You change, even ever so slightly, to keep them safe from harm? If that's what it means, I am there, and I'm more careful and mindful about her well-being than my own.

I take pleasure in every red light stop as she relaxes for a moment, kissing the back of my neck. And I fucking love every time the light switches to green, and her arms tighten again, tethering her to me.

The ride to the beach is entirely too short. Less than thirty minutes later, we arrive at a small patch of deserted sand as the sun hangs low in the sky, preparing for its nightly departure.

Arlo's hands flatten on my stomach, her chest still pressed tight against me as she looks over my shoulder. "It's so beautiful here," she says after I cut the engine.

"I come here to think sometimes," I tell her, looking out over the sand to the Gulf of Mexico with my feet firmly planted on the ground. "It's the best spot to watch the sunset."

She grips my shoulders with her hands as she pushes herself up and off my bike. She runs her fingers through her hair, trying to tame the wildness from the helmet. "It's been a long time since I've come to the beach to watch it."

I climb off, taking her hand in mine, and lead her toward the sand. "I thought this would be a good way to spend tonight. I wanted you all to myself where no one could find us."

She squeezes my fingers, peering at me over her shoulder. "It's perfect," she says softly, her voice nearly drowned out by the crashing of the waves across the sand.

Halfway between the road and the water, I stop and plant my ass in the sand, pulling Arlo down with me.

Her back melts against my front with her hair blowing in the wind and her locks licking my face. This is a small slice of heaven in the middle of nowhere, with no one and nothing around us to interrupt.

"Are you comfortable?" I ask her, sliding my arm over her shoulder, holding her across the top of her chest.

She looks back, a smile gracing her perfect lips. "Very."

"I'm sorry about my cousins last night. It wasn't how I wanted the evening to go."

"It's okay. It was nice to see your entire family isn't perfect."

I laugh, brushing my lips across her neck. "They're not perfect, sugar. Far from it. They're just good at keeping their shit under lock and key."

"I guess we all have our family secrets," she whispers, staring out at the fluffy clouds where they kiss the horizon, the sun peeking out every so often.

"I know they seem cool, calm, and collected, but when shit goes sideways, they're all animals."

Arlo chuckles in my arms, tipping her head back to rest on my shoulder, giving me complete access to her neck. "I can't imagine them that way."

"Stick around long enough, and you'll see for yourself."

"Mello?" she whispers.

I freeze, my lips planted firmly against her skin, and my stomach plummets from her tone. "Yeah?"

"Are you happy?" she repeats my question to her back to me.

"Completely," I answer with no hesitation.

I don't remember the last time I was this happy, but I know it was before the wreck. Afterward, nothing tasted as sweet or felt as good until Arlo walked into my world, turning everything upside down.

"You sure?"

I tighten my arm around her upper body, snaking my other one over her abdomen. "Absolutely, sugar."

There's a comfortable silence between us as I nip at her neck but keep my eyes on the horizon. Arlo is the first woman I've ever been with who doesn't need to fill the silence with words, and my mind is still and peaceful.

"Are you okay after talking to my dad?"

I'd given Arlo time alone with my father, letting her confide in him what she wanted to about her past.

"Your dad is easy to talk to, Mello. He's a great listener, like you."

I smile against her skin. "I haven't always been."

"Shocking," she teases. "But yes, I felt like a weight had been lifted after talking to him. He said he'd do whatever he could to find my birth parents."

"Ar?"

"Yeah?"

"Why did your parents name you Arlo? Were they hippies or something?"

She shrugs. "They loved sixties music. They named me after Arlo Guthrie. It would've been nice if they'd named me after a woman, like Janis Joplin or something, but…"

"It's unique and fits you perfectly."

"I guess so, but I got into a lot of fights as a kid for having a different name."

"Has anything in life been easy for you?"

“This,” she whispers. “This has been easy.”

“Besides us.”

She lifts her head and stares at the water. “My face made things *easier*, but not easy, and besides that, nothing has been even close to easy since my parents died.”

I hold her a little tighter, wishing I could take away all the bad that’s touched her. “I never realized I took my family for granted until I met you. I mean, I knew I was lucky, but I didn’t understand how lucky I’ve been. I’m so sorry, Arlo.”

“It’s normal, Mello. I don’t want anyone to know what it feels like to have no home and for the only family you’ve ever known to die or be taken from you. Be thankful you’ve had the life you had. I would give anything to have grown up surrounded by all the goodness of your family.”

“I am blessed.”

“Your face doesn’t hurt either,” she says with a hint of laughter. “You could’ve been a model.”

I scrunch my nose. “I would’ve been a shit model, babe. It ain’t in me to smile.”

“You would’ve nailed the moody, brooding photo shoots. You have that look down pat.”

I playfully bite down on the tight muscle between her neck and shoulder, and she giggles, squirming against my dick.

“I don’t have a moody look.”

Her hands come up to my arms, holding on to me and giving in to the way my mouth moves against her neck. "You are a mood unto yourself," she tells me, continuing to laugh.

I was right about what I said not that long ago about Arlo. She isn't the type of woman you forget or wipe clean from your soul after she works her way inside. She's unforgettable, leaving an imprint with her sweet laughter, kind smile, and stormy eyes.

"Five years from now, where do you see yourself?" I ask her, fishing for information.

We haven't been dating long…real dating…but I know I can't picture a future without her somewhere in it. Even if she no longer wanted to be with me, I'd have to find a way to keep her as a friend, even if it means seeing her happy with someone else.

"Sitting right here like we are now," she breathes out with a small smile. "You?"

My heart skips and then picks up the pace, her words finally seeping in deep. "Same," I whisper against her neck. "Are we fucked up?"

"Maybe, but if we are, I don't want to be normal."

"Normal has never been my thing," I tell her.

"Do you want kids?" she asks, getting into the nitty-gritty of what the future could look like.

"Do you?" I ask her, wanting to know her answer first.

"I do. Lots of kids."

I swallow. Fuck. Lots? What's her idea of lots of kids, because I don't know if I could handle ten little versions of me or her running around the house? Having a daughter who's half as beautiful as Arlo would be sheer and utter torture. I'd probably spend my golden years behind bars for beating the piss out of some handsy man wanting to get into her pants. "How many?"

"Three or four."

I breathe a sigh of relief. I could handle three or four little people, max. But any more and life would be too busy, and I enjoy our time alone. My parents were insane with the three of us, but somehow, they still managed to make time for each other, never losing their connection.

"I'd be good with that."

"But for now, I want to enjoy us," she says softly into the breeze.

I lean back, taking her with me as the sun kisses the top of the water and the sky explodes into shades of red, orange, pink, and blue.

"It's heavenly, isn't it?" she asks.

"There's only one thing more beautiful."

She smacks my arm. "You don't have to say those things. You already got me, Mello."

I dip my head, bringing my lips near her ear. "Sugar, you're the most beautiful creature I've ever met, and

I'm not just talking about your face or your banging body."

"My banging body?" She laughs again.

"Yep. I said what I said."

"You're crazy."

"Crazy for you," I whisper.

She turns in my arms, sliding her legs underneath mine so our middles are practically touching. "I need to tell you something, but I need you to listen to me before you get mad."

My stomach drops and knots, because there's no smile on her face. Whatever she's about to say is something I won't like or I'm probably not ready to hear. I can tell by the look in her eyes.

"Okay," I say, drawing out the word, bracing myself for maximum devastation.

A minute ago, we were talking about a future and kids, and now she wants to drop a bombshell on me to rock whatever calm we had going.

She reaches up and places her hands against my face. "Promise you'll listen."

I swallow, locking my eyes with hers. "I promise." My entire body is frozen, and I'm barely breathing, too scared to allow myself to relax.

"I don't know how to say this…"

"Just say it, Arlo. Don't dance around whatever it is."

She takes a deep breath and closes her eyes for a

second as she slides her hands to my neck. When her eyes open again, they're soft but filled with sadness. "I haven't been completely truthful with you."

I inhale sharply, feeling like someone just gave me an elbow to the gut. "What?"

She looks down, and I stare at her in complete shock. "I couldn't tell you the truth before. Not because I didn't trust you, but I thought you'd think differently about me."

My hands, which have been at her sides, tighten on her waist. "You couldn't tell me the truth about what?"

She shakes her head, lifting it just enough to look at me through her eyelashes. "I've never told anyone the truth." Tears flood her green eyes, hanging on her lids, ready to fall as she stares up at me. "No one knows, Mello. No one. Not even Lily. You need to promise me what I'm about to say doesn't go beyond us."

"I promise, babe. Nothing you say will go beyond us and this place."

When she gives me her eyes again, the tears are slowly streaming down her cheeks. "Do you know anything about foster homes?"

"I know very little and then what you've told me."

"They're not all rainbows and sunshine. It's rare that one is a happy home where a kid is welcomed and made to feel like a member of the family."

I grab her hand, comforting her, wishing I could wipe away her hurt.

"When I was fifteen, I was moved to a new home, and that's about the time I started getting tits and an ass. And tits and ass get you attention even if you don't want it."

Bile rises in my throat, and my stomach twists. I know what she's going to say before she says it, and the reality of the massiveness of my earlier dickish behavior slams into me. "Arlo," I whisper.

"I was there a month. Only a month, but in that time, my *foster brother* tried to get into my pants nightly. And one time, he succeeded."

"Arlo, sugar," I whisper again, reaching for her, but this time, it's she who moves out of my grip.

"No," she snaps, standing and taking a few steps away. "I've never told anybody this, besides my therapist. And I'm only going to say it once, and then I'll never repeat it again." Her fingers swipe against her cheeks, wiping away the tears. "I fought him off for days and days, but then I got the flu. I was weak, and he knew it. He was the predator, and I was the prey, but I was helpless against his strength with my fever. He forced himself on me, Carmello. He stole something from me that I could never get back."

"I'm sorry," I whisper, watching the girl I've fallen for come apart, telling me her most private and darkest secret. "I'm so, so sorry, Arlo."

"Don't," she bites out. "It wasn't your fault. It

wasn't my fault. I know that now, but it took me a long time to realize I wasn't to my fault."

I stay silent, letting her talk.

"After that, I decided I'd never give a man that part of me again unless I planned on being with him forever. It took me a lot of therapy and a lot of years before I could do anything more than kiss another human being. Although I'm not technically a virgin, in my head, I am. I didn't consent to him forcing himself on me. I didn't ask for him to have sex with me. I didn't want any of it. But when I do give myself to someone, I want it to be because it was my choice and what I wanted and for no other reason. It's easier to tell people I'm a virgin and have them mock the absurdity of that at my age than to tell them the truth."

"You are a virgin, Arlo. You were forced to do something against your will. Virginity isn't taken. It's offered, and you didn't give it to him or anyone."

She crumples to her knees in front of me, finally touching my arm to hold herself up. "Do you hate me?" she whispers, her tears falling harder and faster than before.

I wipe them away, and more replace them before my hand has a chance to move back to the apple of her cheek. "Sugar, no one will ever hurt you again. I promise you that. I'd rather die than let another soul make you cry. Even if you don't want me anymore, I'll always look out for you and protect you. I give you my word that I'll always be there."

She stares at me, the faint glow of the sunset reflecting in her tears, her green eyes somehow greener and more vibrant. "If I want you?" she whispers.

I nod. "Maybe this is going too fast for you."

"If I want you?" she repeats again, her eyes still sad and brimming with tears. "Carmello, I wouldn't have told you if I didn't want you."

"But…" I swallow, hating myself.

She shakes her head. "No." She moves her hands up my arms, bringing them to a rest on my biceps. "I want you. I want what we talked about. I want the five years. I want the kids. I want your family. I want all of it, but I need to know you want me. I need to know you can deal with the reality that's been my life, when you've had the fairy tale every kid dreams about having. I'm damaged, Carmello. Maybe too damaged to be in your life."

"Don't say that." I grab her face, cradling her cheeks gently in my hands. "I'm falling in love with you, Arlo. I want you in my life. I want the five years, the kids, the fairy tale that we create. If anyone's damaged, it's me, babe. I'm the one who's fucked up, not you. I want the forever. The happily ever after. I want to keep every bit of you to myself and only for myself."

"You're falling in love with me?" she whispers, her eyes locked on mine, shining bright in the final remnants of the sunlight.

“I fell, babe. I already fell,” I whisper back.

“But we barely know each other.”

“My dad always said I’d know when I met the person I was meant to be with, and he was right. We can dance around the fact that we were made for each other, or we can jump in and start living our lives, building the happiness we both want and deserve. It’s okay if you don’t feel the same, but—”

I don’t get the words out before her mouth is on mine, kissing me deep and hard. I kiss her back, losing myself in the taste of her lips and the smell of her skin until the air cools, the sky darkens, and time no longer matters.

I officially have Arlo, and nothing else matters, including our pasts.

22

I TAKE THE ENVELOPE MY FATHER GAVE ME FROM THE side table, watching Arlo as she grabs a bottle of water from my fridge.

She spent the entire day writing, while I drew a few custom designs I've been putting off for clients I have booked later this week.

If I had told her about the contents earlier, she would've pushed her work aside and come over right away. But I didn't do that, because I knew she was already behind and starting to stress out.

And after yesterday, I wanted her to focus on something happy, and her writing gives her that. I'm not sure what is inside the envelope, only knowing it is information about her parents.

She glances over her shoulder like she can feel my

eyes on her. “What?” she asks as she turns around with the water in her hand.

“Come here, sugar,” I tell her, patting the couch next to me.

She doesn’t move at first, staring at me, and her gaze dips to the envelope. Finally, she heads my way, her footsteps slow as she makes her way to the couch. “What’s wrong?”

Yesterday at my grandparents’, Arlo had spoken to my father about *possibly* finding her parents for her. But Dad being Dad, he hadn’t waited for her to give the go-ahead before he’d started digging.

“My dad stopped by earlier and dropped this off for you.” I hold out the envelope to her, but she doesn’t take it.

Her eyes are locked on the big brown envelope as she sits. “What’s in it?” she whispers.

“My dad said he found info on your parents and wanted you to have it ASAP.”

Arlo’s eyebrows rise, and I expect her to snatch the envelope from my grip, but instead, she’s completely still. “He did?”

Arlo had given him as many facts about her early childhood as she could remember, but she couldn’t remember much.

“Yeah, Ar.” I push the envelope closer to her. “Here.”

"What's it say?" she asks, finally reaching out and taking it from my hands.

"I didn't read it, sugar. It's not my business."

She runs her hand down the outside of the envelope like she's trying to feel if the news is good or bad without having to open it. "Your dad didn't tell you?"

I shake my head.

She chews on the side of her bottom lip, holding the envelope with both hands. "I don't know if I want to know. What if it's bad news, Mello? I can't take more bad in my life."

I place my hand on her knee, giving it a reassuring squeeze. "Dad didn't say, but I'm sure if it were bad news, he would've given me a hint so I could be prepared."

"I always dreamed of this day, but now I'm scared." She pushes the envelope back my way. "You open it."

My eyebrows furrow. "Me?"

She nods. "Yeah. If it's bad news, you can break it to me in that sweet way you have, instead of me reading the words in black-and-white."

Fucking great. I understand what she's saying, but I don't want to possibly deliver news that would break her heart forever.

"You sure?" I ask, praying she'll change her mind.

"Please." She retracts her hands like the paper burned her, shaking her head slowly. "I can't."

I stare at her, studying her green eyes. "Whatever

you want," I tell her, but my stomach knots at the very possibility that the news I'm going to have to deliver to her will be devastating.

She's had a relatively shitty life—at least, her childhood had been.

She hugs herself, running her hands up and down her upper arms. "Thank you," she whispers.

I undo the metal clasps, peeling back the flap and sliding out the few sheets of white paper inside.

As I scan the first sheet, the second line jumps out at me. "They're alive."

"Oh, thank God." She exhales the breath she's been holding, and then her shoulders slump forward.

I keep reading, skipping over bits and skimming the document before reading the words to her.

Mother: Alena Costas

Location: Chicago, IL

Alena Costas married David Howell twenty years ago and has resided in the Chicago area since birth. She's a nurse at Rush Memorial, working in the ICU for the last ten years. Alena and David have no children together, and there's only one birth on record for Alena. She gave birth to a female child by the name of Karisa Delizonas.

I peer up to find Arlo barely breathing and clutching her chest.

"My name's Karisa?"

"That's what she put on your birth certificate, baby."

"Is there more?"

I squeeze her hand and continue.

Father: Adrian Delizonas

Location: Chicago, IL

Adrian Delizonas has been married to Karen Black for the last seventeen years. They live near Greektown and run a successful restaurant that has been passed down in the family for the last fifty years. Adrian and Karen have two children, both under the age of ten.

It's unclear the relationship Adrian and Alena had in their youth, but both were under the age of eighteen when Arlo was born.

When contacted, the adoption agency in Chicago provided a note left in the file, stating both the mother and father had contacted the agency, trying to find any information they could about the baby they gave up almost three decades ago.

The agency had very little information to give the birth parents due to the adoption and later death of baby Karisa's parents. They did leave a letter sent by the birth parents inside the file in case Karisa ever contacted the agency. Letter is enclosed.

Arlo's fingers are wrapped around my hand so tightly, my fingertips are tingling. "You okay?" I ask her.

"I don't know what I am."

"Do you want to read the letter?"

She stares at me with those striking green eyes. I see

so much fear mingled with curiosity behind them. If I were in the same situation, I don't know what I'd do.

"I don't know," she whispers as I hold the envelope with the name *Karisa* written on the outside in the most beautiful cursive. She moves closer, placing her head against my shoulder, and stares at the envelope. "What if they never want to see me?"

"But what if they do?" I tell her, kissing the top of her dark-brown hair.

She sucks in a deep breath before relaxing. "I don't know if I'm ready for more."

My phone vibrates on the armrest next to me.

"Answer it," she says as she takes the few sheets of paper from my hands.

I glance at the screen, letting Arlo read the file for herself.

Gigi: Mello, you ever going to fess up about what really happened with my sisters yesterday?

Me: I don't know what you mean.

Pike: Wrong move, brother.

Gigi: They didn't sleep over at your place for no reason. I'm not stupid. My parents may believe their bullshit, but I don't.

Me: They were fine. They were responsible.

Gigi: Meaning they were white-girl wasted?

Me: No. They were not.

Gigi: One of them was.

Me: I'll talk to you about it next time I see you.

Gigi: I expect answers, but they're not talking.

Me: Some things are better left unsaid, Gigi.

Gigi: Not in my world.

Pike: That shit's the truth.

Mammoth: <dying>

Gigi: Shut it.

Jett: Pike doesn't want to get laid for a long, long time.

Nick: Cold, brother. Ice fucking cold.

Gigi: I'm done with y'all.

Tamara: Sit on his face and suffocate him to death.

Pike: Is that supposed to be punishment?

Arlo takes my phone, placing the papers on the couch next to her, and scrolls through the messages after I start laughing. "I love your family," she says with a sigh.

"Why? They're messed up. Can't you see that?"

"That's what makes them so great. You have a group chat. Do you know how amazingly lucky you are to have that?"

"Do you know how hard it is to get any sleep with them chattering all hours of the day and night?"

"I'd give up some sleep to have a tribe."

I bend my head, placing my face in her neck. "My tribe is your tribe now, sugar."

"I'll know I've made it once I'm in the chat."

"I'll add you now."

“No,” she says immediately. “I don’t want a pity add.”

“What the hell is a pity add?” I ask her, confused.

“I want to be added because people want me there, not because my big mouth said something.”

“They want you.”

“No, they don’t.”

“The girls will want you. They’re outnumbered right now.”

“Does everyone keep gender score in your family?”

“Basically,” I murmur against her skin. “And I’m the only one not married in this chat. They took pity on me and allowed me in the chat because Rocco’s my twin or else I wouldn’t even be in it. It sucks when there’s no one to have my back.”

She turns and sits up, facing me. “Your brother always has your back.”

“Not when Rebel’s involved and thinks differently from me. Wife trumps brother.”

Arlo laughs. “I’ll never make you choose.”

“You will, and I’ll happily take your side over his.”

She blinks, her laughter dying. “Why?”

“Because he isn’t the one who will be sleeping next to me, sugar.”

She smiles and my heart flutters, the same feeling Arlo’s given me since I laid eyes on her. “You’re silly. There’re no sides if we’re all family.”

I pull her forward, bringing her lips close to mine.

"You have so much to learn, Arlo. So much to learn. But don't worry, babe. I'll teach you all the things."

"What kinds of things?" she asks playfully, batting her beautiful dark eyelashes.

"Anything you want, including all the dirty things." I waggle my eyebrows, pulling her in closer, going for a kiss.

"Will you show me how to do that thing with your mouth?"

"What thing would that be?" I raise an eyebrow, liking where she's going with this.

"The one where you put your lips on me and make my toes curl." She smirks, staring into my eyes with nothing but mischief.

"Does my girl want her world rocked?"

"Your girl wants an orgasm," she answers honestly.

I move forward, pushing her back into the couch and covering her with my body. "Whatever my girl wants, she gets," I tell her before I take her mouth with mine.

Her fingers slide up my biceps and glide under the sleeves of my T-shirt, anchoring herself to me. She kisses me back, moaning into my mouth as I press my dick against her middle, knowing how much she loves to have her pussy touched.

I ache for her, wanting nothing more than to plunge my dick deep inside her. But I also know it won't happen until she is emotionally ready, and I am okay with that too.

Our tongues move together until I pull my head back, pushing myself down her body and taking her pants with me, leaving her bottom bare.

I don't go in for the kill right away. I kiss her stomach, sweeping my lips across her abdomen, worshiping every inch of her body I can until she's squirming underneath me.

Using my hands, I push her legs apart, opening her to me. Her knees fall to the sides, and she lifts her bottom off the cushion, wanting more than I've given.

Even with her open, I don't go straight for her clit. I kiss around her legs, nipping at the skin that makes her moan until she chases my mouth, looking for more.

"Mello," she breathes, reaching down and sliding her fingers into my hair. "Stop teasing me."

I bury my face in her pussy, sucking and licking every inch of her, teasing her clit and making her ass rise and fall with each stroke.

It doesn't take long before her muscles seize, and her breathing grows harsher as the orgasm starts to build. Her thighs clamp shut against my face, suffocating me in her pussy, and if I die now, I'll die a happy man. I don't stop. I don't let up. I suck harder, taking her clit into my mouth and flicking it with my tongue until she's screaming my name, twisting her body through the pleasure.

I pull myself up, curling her into my side as she lies there, spent. She sags into me, still breathing heavy.

"Do you want to talk about…"

"No. I just want to lie here in your arms."

"Whatever you want, babe. Whatever you want."

A few minutes later, Arlo's body stills and her breathing deepens. I pick up my phone and continue the conversation with my family.

Me: What do you think about adding Arlo to the conversation?

Lily: Yes!

Gigi: Fuck yeah.

Tamara: Abso-fucking-lutely

Jo: Do it.

Rebel: Balance of power is shifting.

Pike: It's always been shifted.

Mammoth: Pussy always rules.

Tamara: Smart man.

Rocco: The man finally has his head out of his ass. When's the date?

Me: The date?

Rocco: For the wedding, dumbass.

Me: There's no wedding.

Rocco: There better be. Do not let that one get away.

Me: It's been weeks, brother. Weeks.

Pike: Time is irrelevant when it comes to love.

Me: Weeks.

Mammoth: You want any other women?

Me: No.

Jett: Put a ring on it.

Me: But what if it's too early?

Gigi: Half of marriages end in divorce no matter how soon you get married. Stop being a pussy and just do it, cousin.

Me: You're really inspirational, Gigi.

Gigi: I'm just keeping shit real.

Lily: Either you do it, or someone else will.

Me: I'm not rushing things.

Tamara: Life's too short to go slow.

Me: I don't know how adding someone to a group text turned into marriage.

Rebel: Want us to go ring shopping with you?

Me: No.

Rocco: That's my territory.

Lily: I'm adding Arlo. No more marriage talk. Got it.

Jett: Yes, mama.

Pike: Whatever.

Mammoth: Got it.

Rebel: Lips are sealed.

Rocco: Congrats, brother.

Jo: Noted.

Gigi: I'm not talking.

Tamara: You're always talking.

Gigi: Shut up.

Arlo added to the chat scrolls across my screen, and I smile.

Me: Night, assholes.

With those words, I turn off my notifications and place my phone on the coffee table, relaxing back into the couch and closing my eyes.

"I MADE A DECISION," Arlo says as we sit on the patio overlooking my treelined backyard early the next morning.

"And what's that, babe?"

The letter that was left in her file is on the table between us, still untouched.

"I'm not ready to contact my birth parents."

"Whatever makes you happy. I stand behind you no matter what."

She smiles and takes a sip of coffee before wrapping both hands around the mug. "For the first time in my life, I feel happy. Content, even. The last thing I want to do is to rock the boat. I want to enjoy this feeling for a little while before anything else changes."

"When you're ready, if you ever are, I'll be with you every step of the way to hold your hand."

Her smile widens, almost kissing her eyes. "I know you will, and I love you for that."

"Ditto, babe. Ditto."

23

My mother pulls me aside. "When are you going to ask her?"

I stare at her with my eyebrows pulled down in the middle. "Ask her what?"

She smacks my arm. "To marry you," she says with an eye roll.

I jerk my head back, widening my eyes. "What?"

"I see the way you look at her, and a woman like her doesn't stick around forever, waiting for their man to put a ring on their finger."

I move closer, making sure no one in the house can hear us easily. It's Sunday, and the house is louder than normal since everyone's inside because of a weird winter system dropping torrential rain. "Ma, we've been together weeks."

"So?" she replies, crossing her arms and oozing attitude. "If you know, you know. Do you know?"

"I know, Ma. I know, but I don't think Arlo's ready."

"She's ready." Ma smiles, glancing over at Arlo as she sits with Tamara, Gigi, Lily, Rebel, and Jo. "She's one of us now. Lock her down, and lock her down tight."

"I want to do it when we're ready."

"You're wasting time, son. I see the way you look at her, and I know you're gone. Never seen you look at anyone the way you look at Arlo. Time has a way of getting away from us, moving faster with each passing day. We never know what tomorrow's going to bring, so get a move on it. And I want more grandbabies before I'm too old to enjoy them."

It's my turn to roll my eyes. "You're ridiculous."

"Ridiculously old," she mutters. "And getting older every day. I want more babies before I'm using a walker to get around."

My lips flatten, and I glare at her. "Your crazy guilt isn't going to work on me, Ma."

"What are you two talking about?" Aunt Fran asks, scaring the shit out of us. She's so small, neither of us saw her sneak up on us, listening in on the conversation. "Are you popping the question?"

I hang my head, letting out a deep breath. "Can it be my idea instead of everyone else's?"

"Oh. You *are* going to pop the question." Fran grabs

me around the middle with one arm and squeezes me with her wicked-weird strength.

"When I'm ready."

"There's no time like the present. One day, you're young, and then, *poof,* you're old."

"Fucking crazy people," I mumble under my breath.

"You'll see, sweetie," Fran says, still holding on to me. "We were all young once, and it goes by in a flash. A woman like Arlo, one with no tribe of her own but fitting in with a new one, wants and needs the stability and knowledge that she'll always have a home. If you love her, put a ring on her finger before you do something dumb and lose her forever."

I turn my eyes toward my great aunt. "Why would I do something dumb?"

She shrugs. "You're a man with a penis. They always do something dumb."

"What's going on?" Aunt Angel asks, coming up to join us. "What's the secret?"

"Mello is going to ask Arlo to marry him," Fran tells her.

I lift my hand, scrubbing it down my face. "Why don't we tell everyone?" I mutter.

"Ask her now, and you won't have to tell anyone because everyone will see," Angel says as if it's that simple.

"I haven't even told her I love her yet."

All three women recoil as if I've said something utterly insane.

"What?" my mother whispers in a growly tone.

"Are you crazy?" Aunt Angel says.

"Idiot. All a bunch of idiots," Fran mutters.

Ma reaches out and touches my arm. "Do you love her?"

"I do, more than anything."

She gives my arm a light squeeze. "Then you need to tell her and then put a ring on that finger."

"I want it to be special," I say.

"It doesn't matter how you ask or where, sweetie, but you need to do it before she starts to think you're never going to get to that point. She knows about your history, your lack of commitment, and you don't want any doubt creeping into her mind."

I glance over at Arlo as she's laughing with my cousins. "She doesn't look like she has any doubt."

"She's surrounded by married women who have their place in this family solidified. Eventually, maybe not today or tomorrow, but soon enough, that seed of doubt will be planted, and you don't want it to grow roots."

"What's wrong?" my grandmother asks, coming into the conversation late and unable to stop herself from knowing what we're talking about.

"We're talking about Carmello asking Arlo to marry him."

My grandma smiles. “She belongs here.”

“I need time to find a ring. It has to be perfect.”

My grandmother lifts her hand, working her engagement ring from my grandfather off her finger. “Give her this,” she says, holding it up to me.

I blink, staring at her. “Gram, that’s your ring.”

She pushes it closer to my face. “I know, sweetheart, but I want you and Arlo to have it.”

“But…but…” I stammer, unable to move. “Shouldn’t it go to the oldest or one of the girls?”

“It’s my ring, and I get to decide. Arlo’s a woman without a family, and what’s more welcoming and important than her knowing she’s part of our family by having my ring that your grandfather gave to me all those decades ago. It brought us great luck and so much love. I want to pass it on to you and her so it brings you the same.”

Gram doesn’t wait for me to take the ring. She grabs my hand, placing the platinum and diamond ring in my palm and closing my fingers around it.

“Doesn’t matter when you ask, but don’t wait too long, sweet boy. I need more great-grandbabies.”

“Gram,” I whisper, unfolding my fingers and glancing at the beautiful ring. “I don’t know what to say.”

She touches my face, placing her palm against my cheek. “You don’t need to say anything. Just love her deeply and forever. You had a rough start, my boy, and you deserve happiness for the rest of your years."

I grab her, lifting her off the floor in a hug. "I love you, Gram. So, so much. I don't know how to thank you."

"I love you too, baby, and thank me with babies. Lots of babies."

I place her feet back on the floor and kiss her soft cheek. "Got it, Gram. I'll do my best."

She pats my side. "I know you will," she says with a wink.

"What trouble are you stirring up?" Dad asks, standing behind my mother.

Ma sways backward, leaning her body weight against him. "Mello's in love, James."

Dad bends his neck, looking down at my mom the same way he's looked at her my entire life. There's nothing but love in his gaze, the same way I look at Arlo. "You just figuring that out?"

She lifts her arm, smacking him on the shoulder with the back of her hand. "I knew. I just can't believe it. He's going to ask her to marry him."

"Whoa. Whoa. Whoa. I need a little more time. I still have to tell her I love her."

Dad lifts his head up, staring at me as he wraps his arms around my mother's middle. "You better get on that. Stop wasting time, son."

I shake my head, over family time for this week. "I know. I know. I already had the entire lecture."

"You take that woman home, tell her how you feel, and put a ring on her finger," he tells me like it's that easy. "And in case you're wondering, it is that easy."

It's like the old man can read my mind, which is scary but not entirely surprising since we're so much alike. "I'll remember that as I'm about to piss myself."

My mother rolls her eyes. "You're ridiculous. Now, go sit by your woman and leave us old people be."

I glance over toward the table and catch Arlo's eye. She smiles, her entire face lighting up as she looks at me.

"Go," Gram says, pushing me toward Arlo. "I have to get dessert ready. Leave the women be."

"You mean you have gossip to share. You know it's not about the cake," Dad says, earning himself a single raised eyebrow from my grandmother.

"Oh boy," Aunt Angel says as I walk away, leaving him to get his ass handed to him by the women in the family.

"Hey," Rocco says, catching me before I make it to the table. "You okay?"

I let out a breath. "I just got hijacked by Mom, Gram, Aunt Fran, and Aunt Angel about putting a ring on Arlo's finger."

He laughs. "Welcome to the special type of hell, but

trust me, even once you do it, it doesn't get better. Then they start about the babies."

"Already figured that out."

"We've entered a whole new level," he says.

"Bound to happen eventually."

"You going to ask her?"

"Of course, but she may say no."

He tips his head back and laughs before slapping his big meaty hand on my shoulder, giving it a squeeze. "She isn't going to say no."

"I don't think so either, but damn, what if she does?"

"She won't."

"But…"

He shakes his head. "I'm telling you, she won't, and I'm never wrong."

"You're always wrong," I say with a hint of laughter.

"I never thought you'd find someone to make you happy, but I can sense a calmness and serenity I haven't seen in you for over a decade."

"It's been a long road."

"Tell me about it. I didn't think we'd ever get past that day."

"But we did," I tell him. "Somehow."

"That's what the love of a good woman does," he says, squeezing my shoulder one more time before dropping his hand back to his side. "I want to be the first one to know when you ask her."

"As soon as I tell her I love her."

He raises his face toward the ceiling and shakes his head. "He's a dope."

"I didn't want to rush things."

"Still a dope. Do it tonight and stop being a pussy."

"No talking about this in the chat or to anyone. You hear? They all talk, and I don't want Arlo to get wind of this through a group text message."

"I'll spread the word."

"Don't spread shit," I tell him. "I'm serious. Not a freaking word to anyone."

"You better make it quick then because you told the Gallo family party line between Gram, Fran, and Mom."

"Fuck," I mutter, knowing he's right. "I'll do it tonight."

"Smart man. You got this," he says, being supportive as he always is.

There's something special about having a twin. Something very few people will ever understand. Our bond is solid and strong, a link that can never be severed, no matter what happens. He is the one person I know will always be in my life, but now I know there's another one…Arlo.

24

I'VE PACED A PATH IN THE HARDWOOD FLOOR FOR THE last hour as Arlo typed away on her laptop, begging me to give her some time to finish her novel. She's been working nonstop every moment I'm not around to type *The End.* I am proud of her and everything she's accomplished, something most people would never even try to do.

"I did it. Oh. My. God. I did it," she says, walking into the living room, holding the pile of papers about two inches thick. "It's finished." She places the stack on the table before hurling herself into my arms and wrapping her legs around my middle.

"I'm so proud of you," I tell her, holding her tight and spinning us around in a circle to celebrate. "You're amazing, Arlo. Truly amazing."

She leans back, staring me straight in the eyes as her

hands grab my face, planting a giant kiss on my lips. "I love you," she blurts out, saying it like it's something we've said to each other a million times.

"I love you too," I reply, and her eyes widen as the power and weight of my words finally hit her.

"You do?" she asks, her voice soft and quiet.

"I have for a while now, babe. I love you more than anything."

She peppers my face with kisses before planting a long, deep one straight on my lips. I walk forward, her body attached to mine, our mouths locked together. I collapse backward when my legs hit the couch, and she lands on my lap, never breaking the kiss.

When she pulls away, she says, "I've never been happier than I am right now. I don't think anything could make this day any better."

My stomach twists, and I know now's my chance to ask her, hoping she'll say yes and somehow I will, in fact, make her happier than she ever thought possible.

I lift up, taking her weight, and reaching into my back pocket. "Babe," I whisper, feeling the ring between my fingertips. "I know we haven't known each other very long…"

She's silent, but her eyes are on mine, never leaving my face.

"But there's one thing I know. I always want you in my life. Not only do I love you, Arlo, I want you to be mine forever." I lift up the ring, and her eyes dip, widening as soon as she sees the light shimmer off the diamond. "Will you do me the honor of being my wife?"

Her mouth opens and closes, but no words come out. Tears flood her eyes, hanging on the edges, threatening to fall. "You…" she starts to say, but the words die on her lips as the tears begin to fall. "You want to marry me?" she whispers between sobs.

"I want you to be mine forever, babe. I've had a family my entire life, but I've never felt more at home than I am with you."

"Yes! Yes! Oh my God, yes," she says, sobbing louder as I take her hand, sliding the diamond ring onto her finger.

"This is my grandmother's ring. She gave me her blessing and wanted you to have it so you know you're as much a part of the family as any of us, including me. You're not only gaining a man but the entire crazy-ass group."

She throws her arms around me, almost choking me with the force with which she hugs me. "I have a family," she whispers, the tears now falling onto my T-shirt. "You've given me everything I've ever wanted and more."

"Babe," I say, pulling back so I can see her face. I cradle her cheeks in my hands, staring into her eyes. "You're the one who's given me more than I ever knew

I wanted. I can't wait until you're Mrs. Carmello Caldo."

As soon as the words are out of my mouth, her lips are on me again, taking everything as quick as I can give it.

"I want you," she whispers against my mouth. "I don't want to wait."

"Arlo," I say softly, searching her eyes for any hesitation but seeing nothing but happiness and need. "Are you sure?"

"I'm sure, Carmello. I've saved myself my entire life for the man I'd call my husband, and that man is you."

"My wife," I whisper, loving how that sounds on my tongue.

"Forever," she whispers back as I move my mouth to her neck, kissing a trail down to her collarbone.

I stand, Arlo wrapped around me, my lips on her skin, and move us toward the bedroom, wanting to take my time with her and enjoy every inch of her body. I want the experience to be amazing, wiping away the one from her past.

Gently, I set her on the bed and take off my shirt, throwing it to the side.

"You're really something beautiful," she says, watching me with hungry eyes.

I unbutton my jeans and lower the zipper. "Baby, you're the work of art."

She lifts up, removing her tank top before shimmying out of her shorts, having nothing underneath.

The wind is knocked out of me for a moment before I slide between her legs, covering her warm, soft skin with my own.

"Are you sure?" I ask her again, staring into her green eyes.

"Stop asking," she tells me, taking my face in her hands and pulling my mouth to hers. "I want you, Mello. Make me yours."

My lips slide to her jaw, down to her neck, and lazily make their way to her breasts, readying my girl for her first time. I want her to feel pleasure and not pain, thinking nothing more than how beautiful the moment is.

Her legs fall open as I slide my hand down her side to her hip, finding the small tuft of hair I've spent hours burying my face in over the last weeks.

She moans as her knees drop to the sides, pressing into the mattress, opening her for me. Using my fingers, I ready her, knowing this may hurt, and that's the last thing I want her to experience.

She takes my fingers, moving against my hand, chasing the orgasm like she always does. But I don't want her to come on my hand or against my lips. I want to be buried deep inside her when she lets loose, experiencing more pleasure than she's ever experienced in her life.

She groans as I pull my hand away, leaving her panting and wanting more. I reach for a condom, ripping it open with my teeth before rolling it over the tip of my cock and down my shaft.

My lips find hers again, kissing her deep and long, stroking her skin with my hands, waiting until she's almost breathless and wanton.

"Do you want to get on top, babe?"

Her eyes widen as her chest heaves underneath me, her knees bending at my hips. "No. I like this," she replies softly.

The condom slides against her pussy, moving through her wetness with ease. She's ready for me, wanting this as much as I do.

I lift myself up with one arm, taking my cock in my other hand and guiding myself to her opening. Her eyes are locked on mine, watching me as I slowly slide my dick inside her. Inch by inch, her body adjusts and her breathing changes, but her eyes never close or leave mine.

When my cock's all the way inside her, I stop moving, allowing her body to get used to the sensation. She reaches up, taking my face in her hands, and whispers, "I love you."

"I love you too," I whisper back in the quiet room that's only filled with the sound of our breathing and nothing else.

She hooks her arms around my neck, bringing my

lips back to her mouth, and kisses me as I slide out and rock back into her.

I move slowly, savoring every moment of being inside her, our bodies intertwined and tangled together. Our bodies rock against each other until her orgasm rolls through her, tightening her body around mine, causing the pleasure to rocket through my system, stealing every bit of my breath.

In this moment, I know she's mine and I'm hers. Arlo gave me a precious gift, and it wasn't her virginity. It's her love.

EPILOGUE

ARLO

"You look beautiful," Lily says, coming up behind me and placing her hands on my bare shoulders. "I don't think I've been more excited for anyone's wedding since my own."

I smile at our reflections in the mirror. "I never expected any of this." I run my hand down the white silk gown that fits every inch of my upper body like a glove, flaring out at my hips. "I still can't believe I'm getting married today."

"And you're gaining a family," Lily whispers.

"Bitch, you're stuck with us forever," Tamara adds as she stands in front of the other mirror, adding more mascara to her already ridiculously long and lush eyelashes.

"There are worse things," Gigi tells Tamara.

Rebel comes to stand next to Lily. "As someone not

born into the family, I can say there's nothing more wonderful than knowing and feeling like you've found a home, Arlo. You're not just marrying the man. You're marrying the whole insane tribe, including a new sister."

I turn my gaze toward her in the reflection. "I've never had a sister."

"Me either," she says, smiling back at me, "Until now."

The door to the room opens, and Mrs. Caldo steps inside. "Everyone out except Rebel and Arlo," she announces. "We're about to start, and I need a minute to talk with my girls."

My girl.

God, I love the sound of that.

I'd never been anyone's anything until I told Lily I'd help her figure out why Carmello couldn't stay in a committed relationship.

When Lily told me he wanted to settle down and she needed my help, I jumped at the chance to see him again.

Twice, he saved me. Twice, I was too chickenshit to let him know I wanted to see him again. Twice, I failed to follow through on having enough guts to chase after the only man who'd ever helped me without wanting something in return.

But when Lily made it possible for me to see him again, to be a part of his life—even for a brief time—I couldn't say no.

I wouldn't.

I'd done stupid things in my life, but turning down being around a kind and extremely hot man wouldn't be one of them.

Rebel grabs my hand, giving my fingers a squeeze as Gigi, Lily, Jo, Luna, Rosie, and Tamara leave the room. "Breathe," she whispers.

Mrs. Caldo looks drop-dead gorgeous in a strapless red dress with black peep-toe Christian Louboutin high heels. She looks like someone who just walked out of the pages of *Vogue* and nowhere near old enough to have three grown sons and looking forward to being a grandmother again.

"Rebel, honey, you look absolutely beautiful today," Mrs. Caldo says.

"Thanks, Mom." Rebel smiles. "You look so absolutely stunning."

"I just wanted a minute of peace and quiet with you two before the insanity starts. Can you find James and bring him back here for Arlo?" Mrs. Caldo asks Rebel.

Rebel nods. "Of course. I'll go grab him and check on Adaline."

"I just saw her with my mother and Fran. They're having a great time, but she may have learned a few new words that are not exactly church appropriate." Mrs. Caldo laughs.

"Oh Lord," Rebel whispers before rushing out of the doorway and into the church.

"Sweetie," Mrs. Caldo says, opening her arms as she moves my way. "You're absolutely breathtaking. Wait until Carmello sees you in this dress."

I can't wipe the smile off my face as she wraps her arms around me. "Thank you. I can't wait to see him in his suit. He's already so handsome, I'm not sure my heart can take much more."

She pulls back, looking me in the eye. "I want you to know you're no longer alone. Today, you officially become my daughter and James's daughter. I would be honored if you called me Mom or Ma, but if you're not comfortable with it, I'll understand."

"No. No. I'm the one who would be honored to call you Mom. It's been a long time since I've been able to use that word with anyone, and I can't think of a person more deserving of that term either. I can't thank you enough for making me feel so welcomed as a member of your family, Mom."

She smiles, but her eyes tear up. "You'll never be alone again, my darling girl. I know you'll make my son happy, but more importantly, I know he'll make you happy. I hope you have the same long and deep love that James and I have and that it continues to grow over time. Welcome to the family, baby girl."

I hug her back as the warmth of her words envelopes me. "Thank you, Mom. Thank you."

"Now," she says, pulling back again and touching her fingertip to the corner of my eye. "No crying.

You're going to ruin your makeup, and the wedding is about to start."

I laugh and cry at the same time, trying to blot away the tears before they have a chance to cause streaks down my face. "I'm going to cry it all off at the altar."

"We all do. If my son holds it together, it'll be a miracle."

The door opens again, but this time, it's Mr. Caldo, and his imposing form fills the entire opening. "Arlo, baby, you're gorgeous," he says, and I feel those words just as much as I hear them. "Carmello's not going to know what hit him."

Mrs. Caldo walks up to her husband, places her hand on his chest, and lifts her face toward him. Without hesitation, he bends his neck and kisses her lips. My heart melts at the sweetness of the two of them. They have what I want and what I hope I'm getting and will always have with Carmello.

"Don't take too long, darling," she says to him before looking at me over her shoulder one more time with a smile.

"We'll be right out, love," he tells her, holding on to her hand until she's too far away and the distance pulls them apart. "Are you ready?"

I take a deep breath and nod. "I am."

"My son is a lucky man to have someone as kind as you come into his life and love him in return. I want you to know that, no matter what happens, you're not only

Izzy's daughter but mine too. I will always be here for you and help in any way I can. The Gallos welcomed me into their family, and not a day has gone by when I haven't felt wanted and loved. I know it'll be the same for you, Arlo."

I move toward him, careful not to step on my dress. "Can I ask you something?"

He nods.

"Is it wrong that I never contacted my birth parents? I don't know why, but I keep thinking of them today."

He shakes his head and takes my hand. "There's nothing wrong with that. Someday, you may want to contact them, or maybe you never will. You have to do what feels right to you, Arlo. Never let anyone make you feel guilty, especially not yourself."

"I'm happy you're here with me today, Mr. Caldo."

"Can I make one request?" he asks, smiling at me so sweetly my heart aches.

"Always."

"Can you please call me Dad?"

My smile is immediate. "I'd like that."

"Me too," he says softly as he holds out his arm, waiting for me to take it.

I'm thankful for Carmello's father and his willingness to walk me down the aisle. I haven't had a father figure in my life for decades, but he's quickly filled the role, giving out sage advice and always being there when he's needed.

I'm practically shaking as we walk out of the room toward the church where the entire family is waiting, including my husband-to-be.

Mr. Caldo pats my hand, locking his arm tighter with mine to take more of my weight and give me strength. "Breathe, Arlo. There are only good things to come," he tells me. "Your future will be a beautiful thing."

And when the church doors open and I see my husband-to-be waiting at the end of the aisle, standing tall on the altar with a smile, I know my future is going to be more than I ever dreamed it could be.

The Gallos aren't finished...learn more about the next novel in the Men of Inked Family Saga at menofinked.com/next

Learn more at menofinked.com/gallo-saga

FREE EBOOKS

MENOFINKED.COM/FREE-BOOKS

About Chelle Bliss

She's a full-time writer, time-waster extraordinaire, social media addict, coffee fiend, and ex-history teacher.

Join her **Private Facebook Reader Group** at *facebook.com/groups/blisshangout*

Where to Follow Me:

- facebook.com/authorchellebliss1
- bookbub.com/authors/chelle-bliss
- instagram.com/authorchellebliss
- twitter.com/ChelleBliss1
- goodreads.com/chellebliss
- amazon.com/author/chellebliss
- pinterest.com/chellebliss10

Made in the USA
Las Vegas, NV
24 July 2021

26972846R00187